TEA IS FOR TALISMAN

A HAUNTED TEAROOM COZY MYSTERY

KAREN SUE WALKER

ACKNOWLEDGEMENTS

My gorgeous cover was designed by Mariah Sinclair, the Cozy Cover Queen. You can find her at https://www.thecovervault.com or on Facebook.

Thank you to Alyssa Lynn Palmer for your copyediting expertise, and Laura Johnson for catching all the pesky typos!

Many thanks to my wonderful readers, typo catchers, and reviewers. Keep on sending me those emails with suggestions, ideas, and pictures of your cats and dogs!

Sign up for *Karen's Cozy Club* email updates at https://karensuewalker.com and I'll do my best to keep your inbox full of everything cozy.

CHAPTER 1

The problem with ghosts is that you never know when they're listening—or plotting to tag along on your vacation. My assistant Jennifer and I had taken to texting each other about our upcoming trip to New Orleans so George and Pearl, two ghostly vaudeville performers, wouldn't overhear our plans. I'd met the pair while solving a murder in a nearby town, and they'd followed me home like a couple of strays. Now, they were determined to follow us to New Orleans.

If we could get through the weekend without George and Pearl discovering our plans, we might make it to the airport on Monday without any ghostly stowaways.

Jennifer and I sat at the kitchen island, where we spent a good deal of our time. I'd converted the front rooms of my Victorian home into a tearoom, and we lived in rooms on the second floor. I had given Jennifer a special employee deal when her father had kicked her out of his house.

I did my best to focus on last minute details for our monthly, themed afternoon tea. We'd finally chosen the Jane Austen theme Jennifer had her heart set on, complete with Regency outfits, food, and décor. Jennifer took care of planning everything but the food—that was my specialty, though she did have a few suggestions.

"Are we serving seed cakes?" she asked.

"You know the event is tomorrow." I hoped she wasn't asking me to change the menu this late in the game.

"I know. I was just wondering. I didn't mean for you to add them if they're not already on the menu."

"I promise when we get back from our trip, I'll make seed cakes. Maybe you can help me find a recipe."

"Of course!" She jumped up, her ponytail bouncing as she carried her teacup to the sink. "I hope I like them. Am I making you jittery? I am, aren't I? I'm so excited about the Jane Austen tea that I can hardly sit still. I think I'll go in the other room and polish the furniture."

"Good idea." Ever since she'd come to work for me, she'd felt like more of a daughter than an employee. Her youthful enthusiasm energized me, although occasionally it could be a bit overwhelming. I wrapped my hands around my warm teacup and breathed in the warm floral scent of freshly brewed lavender Earl Grey tea which always calmed me.

Nearly an hour later, I looked up from my notebook as Jennifer returned to the kitchen. "What were we thinking, planning a big event right before our trip?" I asked.

"It'll be fine." Jennifer refilled my teacup with the nearly empty teapot, then put the kettle on the stove to boil. "Did you try on the dress I picked out for you?"

"It's perfect, of course. I knew it would be." One of my assistant's hobbies was antique and vintage clothing, and she'd found me a beautiful gown to wear. At fifty, I wasn't sure how I felt about dressing up like a Jane Austen character, but it was all for a good cause.

As I double checked the menu for the event, a familiar tap-tap-tap on the back door piqued my curiosity.

I put down my pen. "That almost sounds like Irma's knock, but she would have told us if she was coming back, wouldn't she?"

"Only one way to find out." Jennifer hurried to the door and threw it open. "It *is* you!"

"Of course it's me." Irma, our 70-something neighbor, leaned her walking stick against the counter and pushed past Jennifer. "Who else would be using my signature knock?"

I jumped up from my seat and held my arms out wide for a hug. "Why didn't you tell us you were coming back today?" A thought popped into my head unbidden. "Is everything okay?"

She ignored my outstretched arms and brushed off my question with a wave of her hand. "Of course. And I did tell you." She paused and pursed her lips. "Didn't I? Oh, well, I meant to."

"No worries." Jennifer pushed a stool in her direction. "You're here now and that's what's important. Would you like a cup of tea?"

Irma's eyebrows drew together. "Is the cappuccino machine broken or something?"

Jennifer took the hint. "I'll make you a mocha." She hurried over to the oversized vintage cappuccino machine and began flipping levers and turning knobs. The ancient machine sputtered to life.

"Are you home for good?" I asked Irma as I returned to my seat at the island.

She rested her elbows on the tile counter. "Zoe didn't want to move to Lavender Falls permanently, so for now, I'm back. Funny how much I missed having my granddaughter around after going years and years not even knowing she existed."

Two months earlier, Irma and I had visited Lavender Falls, a town that seemed straight out of a fairy tale. When I returned, she had stayed behind and considered making a new start there after her pier-side restaurant had been destroyed in a huge storm that spring.

"I'm glad you're back," Jennifer said over the hissing sound of the milk frother.

"You're glad Zoe's not moving away with me,

you mean." Irma's tone was cross, but I spotted the corner of her mouth turning up in a suppressed smile. "You two are thick as thieves."

Jennifer set Irma's mocha in front of her. "Thick as thieves? We're not doing anything illegal."

Irma rolled her eyes like a petulant teenager. "It's just an expression."

"I'm glad you're back for another reason," I said. "I'm hoping you'll help with our Jane Austen event this weekend. Special events are a lot of work."

"Don't I know it. The Mermaid Cafe hosted all kinds of events. They're exhausting, but they can be quite profitable."

"And fun?" Jennifer asked hopefully.

Irma shrugged. "If you like that sort of thing, I suppose. Are you going to make me get all dressed up?"

"I won't *make* you, but I had hoped..." Jennifer gave Irma puppy dog eyes and waited for her to respond.

"Fine. But it had better be flattering. I haven't gotten hit on since I quit wearing my mermaid costume at the cafe."

I snickered, but when she shot me a glare, I managed to turn it into a sneeze.

"Regency era dresses are flattering for all body types and sizes. They're empire style with a high waistline." Jennifer held her hand just under her bust to demonstrate. "And they're loose and flowing down to the floor, so they hide any flaws."

"Who said I had flaws?" Irma asked.

"Not me." I smiled at my crochety friend, surprised how much I'd missed her. "You're like Mary Poppins. Practically perfect in every way."

She peered at me suspiciously. "What else do you want from me, April May?"

I chuckled. "I'm also hoping you can keep an eye on things for a few days next week while I take Jennifer on a mini vacation. It's her first time out of California."

"Where are you two going?"

I dropped my voice to a whisper. "New Orleans."

"Why are you whispering?" Irma leaned forward. "What's so secret about New Orleans?"

"Shhh…" I warned, but it was too late. Pearl and George popped into view, although since they were ghosts, I was the only one who could see them.

Jennifer saw the look on my face. "Uh oh. George and Pearl?"

"Yep."

Pearl looked like she'd stepped out of a 1920s gangster movie, with her flapper dress and bleached blonde bob. George was stylish in a pin-striped suit and red tie. The two ghosts had begun to grow on me since I'd met them months earlier, but I really didn't want them tagging along to New Orleans.

George leaned one elbow on the island. "Hey, doll. So, the getaway is back on?"

I explained to Irma that the two ghosts wanted to come on our trip. "Can you imagine me trying to act normally on an airplane with the two of them doing who-knows-what?"

"We won't cause no trouble," Pearl said, although I knew better. "When we goin'?"

I sighed. "We haven't made a decision yet."

"What do you mean?" Irma asked. "You just said—"

I waved my hands to stop her. "We're going, but we don't know when. We definitely haven't bought our airline tickets or made any hotel reservations or anything like that."

Irma caught on. "Oh, right. The weather will be better in a few months, anyway. Like February."

"Exactly." I turned to Pearl. "I'll let you know the minute we decide."

"You'd better, sister. Or you won't hear the end of it."

CHAPTER 2

*A*fter running her own restaurant for several decades, Irma's expertise and knowledge often came in handy. Sometimes, it also came at a price.

"How about a favor for a favor?" Irma asked. "That's not to say I wouldn't help you out of the goodness of my heart, but as long as you're out of town next week, I wondered…"

Uh oh. "If you can throw a huge bash at my home?"

"No, nothing like that."

"If you can run a restaurant out of my tearoom serving cocktails without a liquor license?" The last time she'd done that, she got both of us in hot water. Luckily, we didn't get in any serious trouble, but only because she gave all the diners their money back. I had hoped she'd learned her lesson.

"I'm thinking about giving some cooking classes from time to time. My little kitchen has barely enough room for Zoe and me, so I thought I could use yours. Maybe on a Friday evening after your tearoom is closed for the day."

"That's it?" I had a good reason for being suspicious of Irma, but she did need something to keep her busy. "As long as you clean up afterwards. And by that, I mean on Saturday morning, there should be no sign that you and your students were ever here."

Irma beamed. "You bet. And… just one more thing. Zoe wants to do a video of me cooking to get people interested. Since you're gone this week, I assume it won't be a problem using your kitchen for that too."

I hesitated. "Is there anything else?"

Irma slipped off her stool, sensing victory. "That's it. I'll go tell Zoe. She's really excited about making the video."

"Of you?" I suppressed a snicker.

She shrugged. "I know, I know. Who wants to watch an old broad like me when you can watch a cute young teeny bopper dancing and wiggling what God gave her? But it's worth a shot."

I'D SOMEHOW CONVINCED SHERIFF ANDREW FONTANA, who I happened to be dating, to act as a host for the Jane Austen event. Part of the reason for the brisk ticket sales might have been the opportunity to see our local sheriff in period costume.

When he walked through the door, he took my breath away. I'd always thought he was handsome, but in a vest, tailcoat, and top hat, he looked positively dashing.

"Colin Firth eat your heart out." I gave him a kiss on the cheek.

"Is that all I get after all the trouble I've gone to?" he teased. "A peck?"

I gave him a long kiss on the lips just as Jennifer came down the stairs in a pale blue empire dress with short puffy sleeves and long white gloves.

"Don't mind me." She shielded her eyes as she passed by on her way to the kitchen. "But you'd better get changed, April."

"I wanted to wait until the last minute, so I didn't spill anything on my dress."

"The event starts in an hour, so I'd say it is the last minute."

"Oh right." I took a moment to give Andy's outfit the admiration it deserved, then excused myself and ran upstairs.

My dress, made from burgundy brushed cotton, had long sleeves puffed at the top. I tucked a sheer white scarf into the low neckline and wound my hair up under a lace cap. Catching my reflection in the mirror, I almost didn't recognize myself.

I'd become a different person—a respected business owner, but more importantly, someone with friends who were like family. Friends, plural. That was a new experience for me, and I had this town and its residents to thank for that.

In the time since I first discovered Serenity Cove, my life had changed dramatically. My days were filled with baking, serving afternoon tea, and spending time with my friends—some of the best friends a girl could possibly have. And a relationship with a wonderful man who came into my life after I'd thought the chance for romance had passed me by.

Soft music wafted up from the first floor, which meant the musicians had arrived and the string quartet was warming up. Everything was coming together perfectly.

I slipped on the white gloves Jennifer had laid out for me and headed downstairs. When I reached the landing, Andy caught sight of me and broke out in a wide smile. He took off his hat and bowed elegantly.

When I reached the bottom of the stairs, he held out his arm for me.

"My lady, you must allow me to tell you how ardently I admire and love you."

"That sounds familiar somehow."

"I confess, I got a copy of *Pride and Prejudice* and highlighted phrases to memorize. However, I disapprove of Darcy's reluctance to dance. I would dance every dance if it were with you. Will you oblige me?"

I curtsied. "I will do my best, but as a young eligible woman with excellent prospects, I'm sure to have many suitors. You may have to challenge one or more to a duel."

"Very well," he grinned. "I was on the fencing team in college, so I feel quite prepared to defend your honor if necessary."

Jennifer emerged from the kitchen and stopped, holding up a hand. "Wait right there." She retreated, emerging a moment later with her phone. "I have got to get pictures of you two. Over here in front of the settee."

Andy's eyebrows rose. "What's a settee?"

"It's a sort of old-fashioned sofa. Jennifer borrowed some furniture from her dad. They used to own an antique shop in town where I first met her. I was looking for vintage teacups and Jennifer was pretending to be a mannequin."

"I was not," Jennifer protested as she posed us by the settee. "I just stand very still sometimes."

After Jennifer had snapped plenty of pictures in several poses, we went over the schedule, as much for me as for them.

"The event starts at two. At around two-thirty, we'll start serving afternoon tea minus the desserts. Those will come later."

"So just scones, sandwiches, and savories?" Jennifer asked.

"Exactly. There's discussion among Regency experts whether scones and clotted cream were served during Jane Austin's time, but I'm not about to serve afternoon tea without scones."

Andy listened intently. "I thought it was called high tea."

"That's a common misconception." I generally

held my tongue when a guest called afternoon tea "high tea," because no one likes to be corrected. But I enjoyed a chance to explain the difference. "High tea was a meal eaten in the early evening, usually by the working classes. It originally got its name because it was served on high tables while afternoon tea was served on low tables, like a coffee table. A lot of people like to say, 'high tea' because it sounded fancy, but in reality, it's the opposite."

"She could go on for hours like this if you let her," Jennifer said with a grin.

"Yes, but right now I need to make sure everything is ready to go in the kitchen. If you," I gave Andy a little curtsy, "will help Jennifer seat the guests, she'll find out what kind of tea they want. We're limiting the selection to four for simplicity's sake."

"There's more than four types of tea?" Andy asked. When he saw the look on my face, he said, "Just kidding. I know there's at least seven or eight."

Jennifer gestured to the dozens of tiny glasses lined up on a nearby sideboard. "What about the elderflower cordial?"

"I nearly forgot. Maybe Andy can help us serve that to the guests as they arrive." I gave him a hopeful smile.

"Glad to be of service." He bowed gracefully from the waist, and I wondered if he'd been practicing.

I retrieved one of the pitchers of homemade

elderflower syrup from the refrigerator, along with a bottle of mineral water, and set it next to the glasses. Then I went back for the sparkling wine.

"Fill half the glass with cordial and top off with mineral water or sparkling wine." I gave the two of them a little smile. "We'd better do a taste test first, don't you think?"

They agreed, and I poured some of the elderflower cordial into three glasses as Andy opened the champagne.

"No alcohol for me," Jennifer said. "At least, not until after the event. I get too sleepy."

I'd just taken a sip of my cordial when Irma arrived, followed by the first guests.

I took a deep breath and announced, "It's showtime!"

CHAPTER 3

As the guests arrived, Jennifer, Andy, and I served them elderflower cordials while the quartet played chamber music. The crowd was a mix of friends, neighbors, and strangers. Some wore authentic Regency clothing, while others cobbled together outfits from Halloween costumes and Renaissance fairs. It made for a colorful and delightful mix.

Several locals had created imaginative themed gift baskets for a silent auction. I'd donated a tea-themed basket that included afternoon tea for two. Sarah and Simon Arvin, owners of the Serenity Cove Bed and Breakfast, generously donated a weekend stay along with their sea-themed basket.

Dr. Fredeline Severs, aka "Freddie," our local doctor, coroner, and a good friend, arrived with three women I hadn't met before. I hurried over to give her a hug and meet her friends. She handed me a huge spa-themed basket filled with self-care items for the auction as Andy led her friends to a table.

I complemented her ice blue gown with chiffon overlay. "You look amazing." What really caught my eye was the pendant she wore.

"It's a talisman I bought on a visit to New Orleans at this little shop called Vampyre Boutique in the French Quarter. I remembered it when you were talking about your vacation, so I dug it out of my jewelry case. I don't think it goes with the outfit, though, do you?"

"Everything looks good on you." I always admired her elegance and style.

Freddie lowered her voice. "The woman who sold it to me said it would bring me good luck. I bought it because I thought it was pretty, but why don't you wear it on your trip? You never know when a little luck might help."

She took the pendant off, then handed it to me before disappearing into the crowd. I turned the oval-shaped charm over in my hand. It appeared to be made of aged copper, its surface etched with intricate swirls and crescent moons. I pulled the delicate brass chain over my head and tucked the talisman under my dress next to my heart.

"Madam," came the voice of Deputy Alex Molina.

I spun around. He and Deputy Timothy "Tiny" Bonner wore full Regency costume right down to silk cravats.

Molina gave me a sly grin. "I hope we won't be finding any dead bodies today."

"Don't even say that!" I said in mock horror, adding in a whisper, "No one's been murdered for months. Let's keep it that way." I gestured to his clothing. "Did the sheriff convince you to wear that?"

Molina grinned and nodded. "He said it was for a good cause."

Jennifer appeared next to me. "All funds go to The Serenity Cove Foundation for Children's Literacy. And you both look amazing."

Tiny seemed relieved that we approved. "It wasn't easy to find a costume in my size."

Deputy Molina tipped his hat and smiled. "Enjoy the event, ladies. We'll keep an eye on things." With a quick bow, he and Tiny moved on, stopping to chat with some of the guests.

To get everyone's attention, I clinked a teaspoon on the side of a glass. "If everyone will be seated, we will begin serving afternoon tea. For those of you who are having afternoon tea for the first time, you are in for a treat. The sandwiches may look small," I glanced at Molina and Tiny, then continued. "But I promise you will not leave hungry."

Jennifer and Irma emerged from the kitchen, each holding two three-tiered stands. I motioned for Jennifer to join me as Irma continued serving.

"Traditionally, you will start with the bottom tier and work your way up, but I'm not going to scold anyone who wants to do things in a different order.

On the bottom," I gestured to one of the trays Jennifer held, "you'll find finger sandwiches, and on the next, bite-sized quiches and puff pastry tarts. There is one per person, but do let us know if you want an extra of one of the items.

"On the top tier," I continued, "are warm scones. These are not the scones you find at your local coffee shop that would be put to better use as doorstops, in my opinion. You may eat them with butter if you like, but I recommend trying them with a healthy amount of clotted cream and jam."

Jennifer whispered. "Tell them about dessert."

"Yes, there will be a selection of desserts after the dance lesson." I paused for effect, noticing several of the men looked like deer caught in head-lights. "Just kidding. Anyone have any questions?"

Tiny raised a tentative hand. "Can we eat now?"

I laughed. "Yes, please enjoy yourselves."

The soft strains of the quartet, the hum of conversations, and the occasional clink of teacups created a warm and inviting atmosphere.

Jennifer stayed in the kitchen plating the dessert trays, while I made sure to keep the teacups full. I soon joined her, bringing with me two teapots to be refilled.

"How's it going?" she asked.

"Smooth so far. I haven't spilled tea on anyone, and no one's fainted from wearing a corset," I joked. "I think this might be our most successful event yet."

As I returned to the tearoom, I paused and

took in the scene. The atmosphere was almost magical, with the afternoon light filtering through the lace curtains, casting a soft glow over the guests.

Irma appeared at my side, breaking the spell. "Do you want me to start wrapping up the silent auction? We've got bids on all the items."

"Yes, let's start closing it out," I agreed. "I'll make an announcement."

Stepping toward the center of the room, I tapped a spoon against a teacup to get everyone's attention. The gentle murmur of conversation died down, and all eyes turned toward me.

"Ladies and gentlemen," I began, "thank you all for attending our Jane Austen-themed afternoon tea. It's been a pleasure hosting you, and I hope you've all enjoyed yourselves as much as we've enjoyed putting this event together. The silent auction will be closing in ten minutes, so if you have any final bids, now's the time!"

Murmurs rippled through the room as guests moved toward the auction table for one last look. I smiled, feeling a sense of accomplishment as the event neared its conclusion. The afternoon had gone off without a hitch—no drama, no disasters, and certainly no dead bodies. That in itself was a victory.

As the auction wrapped up and Irma handed out baskets to the lucky winners, I caught a glimpse of Freddie heading toward the door. I waved to her, and she waved back, mouthing, "Good luck!" as she tapped her chest where the talisman had once rested.

Before long, the guests began to leave, and the lively atmosphere slowly faded into the relaxed comfort of a day well spent. The quartet played their final notes, the soft cadence of the music providing a fitting end to the afternoon.

Jennifer and I stood by the door, thanking everyone as they left. "We hope to see you at the next event."

As the door closed behind the final guest, I instinctively touched the pendant hanging around my neck. There was something oddly comforting about its presence, like a gentle reminder that luck—or something else—might be on our side.

After the last guest left and the dishwasher hummed, Andy and I sat on the porch swing watching the sun slowly sinking below the horizon. A cool breeze carried the salty tang of the sea, bringing with it the rhythmic sound crashing waves.

Pleasantly tired from the busy day, I sipped on a cup of Darjeeling tea, breathing in its subtle floral notes and earthy undertone. I found it both calming and reviving.

Andy took my hand in his. "I like what we have."

"I do too."

"Do you ever think about marriage?"

I nearly spit out my tea, surprised by the question but also by the answer I was about to give. "No, I really don't."

"You know I love you."

I felt a warm glow wash over me. "Yes, I do know." It felt good to say those words. "Why?"

His smile wavered. "Why do I love you?"

I nodded.

"Hmmm…" He looked out at the ocean for several seconds. "I love how you're kind to everyone, even people you don't especially like. I love your loyalty. And I love how you put me on the spot with your questions." His grin told me he was teasing me. "But what I think might be even more important is that I like you."

"You like me? You really, really like me?"

He chuckled. "I do. You're easy to be with. I hope you'll forgive me for bringing up my past. I thought what I had was love. But I always felt like I didn't quite measure up. With you, I feel content. Balanced. Like I can be myself and it's enough."

If that didn't call for a kiss, I didn't know what did. The kiss was like Andy—warm, gentle, and reassuring.

I stared into his kind eyes for a long moment. "I like you, too."

"I can see myself growing old with you. Or maybe I should say 'older,' since I'm not exactly a spring chicken."

"We don't have to be married to do that. Is there something else on your mind that you're asking such serious questions?"

He chuckled. "I was reading *Pride and Prejudice* to get ready for the event, but I kept falling asleep." He gave me a glance. "Don't judge me. Reading always makes me sleepy. So, I watched it on TV—the BBC series, not any of the movies. Jennifer was insistent that the miniseries is the best version."

"She's not wrong."

"And it got me wondering. Marriage was so important to all of them—not just the women, but the men too."

"It was a different time." I took his hand in mine and gave it a gentle squeeze. "I think what we have is about as good as it gets."

"Me too."

As we swung gently back and forth on the porch swing holding hands, I couldn't help but think that the moment was just about perfect.

CHAPTER 4

I tiptoed down the stairs with my suitcase, doing my best to avoid alerting George and Pearl. I carried it out to my car, put it in the trunk, and slammed the lid.

"So far so good," I mumbled to myself as I went back inside.

The moment I stepped through the door, I squealed at the sight of Pearl, who appeared out of nowhere right in front of me. She stood with one hand on her hip.

Her eyes narrowed. "Watcha doin'?"

"Oh, just putting some things in the car to donate. Some old clothes, stuff like that."

She stared as if she knew I was lying. "Funny. Jennifer is in her room putting some clothes in a suitcase too. I suppose you just decided to get rid of them old suitcases?"

"Listen, Pearl." My patience was getting thin. "What I do is my own business. I don't mind if you and George go to New Orleans. In fact, it's a great idea. Go, and have a great time. Just not with us."

She pulled back as if offended. "You don't need to be like that. If you want us to beat it, just say so. We don't need no favors from you."

"Okay, beat it." The look on Pearl's face made me regret my words. "I'm sorry, Pearl, but Jennifer and I have been planning this for months, and I need a break."

Her red lips formed a pout. "Ever think I need a break, sis?"

"No," I answered honestly. "What I think you need is to go to the light. The afterlife promises new adventures for you and George. This world is not your world anymore."

Pearl's mouth dropped open. "I never thought I'd get the bum's rush from you. I thought you was a classy bird, but I guess I got you pegged wrong." She swung around and strutted away, slowly fading until she'd completely disappeared.

Jennifer appeared on the landing with her suitcase and backpack.

She took one look at me and asked, "What's wrong?"

"Pearl." I half expected her to reappear at the sound of her name as she so often did, but not this time. "I told her she needs to go to the light."

"In other words, you told her to get lost."

"In a nice way." My shoulders slumped. "Okay, maybe not that nice, but she and George sure can get on my nerves."

"Yep. I can always tell when they're around because you seem so distracted." She carried her suitcase to the bottom of the staircase. "Looking on the bright side, does this mean they're not coming along?"

"Hopefully not. I don't see why they can't go to New Orleans on their own if they want."

"Do you think they've somehow gotten themselves attached to you? Like psychically or something?"

"Oh my—" I hadn't thought of that before. "I sure hope not."

"Are we ready?" Jennifer asked.

I took in her traveling outfit—a floral fifties-style dress paired with a coordinated sweater and ballet flats before giving myself and my sweatpants a once-over. "I wish I'd worn something nicer now that I see your outfit."

"You look fine," she said, diplomatically. "You look comfortable."

"Here, give me that." I took Jennifer's suitcase, and she followed me to the car.

As I put the suitcase in the trunk, I pondered which was worse—a friendly ghost or an angry one. I'd worry about that when we returned home. In a few hours, I'd be ordering a po' boy or jambalaya in the French Quarter.

"I'm going to do a sweep of the house and make sure all the lights are turned off and the windows are shut."

As I went from room to room, the house felt

eerily quiet. I walked past the door to the attic, a wistful feeling coming over me as I thought about Whisk, who was probably curled up on Zoe's lap at that moment.

As we waited in a huge line to get through security, I spotted George and Pearl and groaned.

"They're here." I didn't need to tell Jennifer who I meant.

Pearl sashayed over to us, a huge grin on her face. "That's too bad you have to stand in this long line. I suppose we could stay with you and keep you company. Help you pass the time."

"That's not necessary," I assured her under my breath.

"Good!" She grabbed George by the arm. "Cuz I'm not hanging around here waiting for you. Airports sure have changed." The two of them slipped past the crowd waiting to go through the metal detectors.

Jennifer seemed edgy, and I tried to reassure her. I'd already coached her about the limits on liquids. "All you have to do is take the plastic bag with your cosmetics out of your suitcase, then put it, your phone, and your shoes in one of those bins. Then you put it on the conveyor belt, and it goes through the X-ray machine. You'll retrieve them on the other side."

"What about my suitcase?" she asked.

"That goes on the conveyor belt too, but not in a bin."

As I slipped my shoes off, George appeared, his face inches from mine.

"Why you takin' your shoes off?" he asked.

"Shhh…" I whispered. "Leave me alone, would you?"

The man behind me said indignantly, "I never touched you."

"Sorry," I murmured. "I was talking to someone else."

A young woman in torn jeans behind him complained, "You're holding things up, lady."

"Sorry." I put my things in the bins and followed Jennifer.

Pearl grabbed my arm and went through the metal detector with me as a loud alarm went off.

The security agent pointed to the phone in my hand. "You're supposed to put that in the bins."

The torn jeans lady sighed loudly as I retreated and set my phone next to my shoes and tried again.

Meanwhile, Pearl kept up a running commentary. "I wouldn't be seen in public looking like that. How come she can afford to go on a trip, but she can't afford a decent pair of trousers. Course, in my day, trousers were for men."

I did my best to tune her out as I held out my arms so the agent could wave her wand over me.

As I finally was cleared to go to our gate, Jennifer helped me gather my things. "What was that all about? You seemed totally distracted."

"Pearl." I threw my bag over my shoulder, grabbed the handle of my suitcase, and we headed for our gate. "She's been giving me her opinions of modern fashion. In short, she doesn't approve."

"I kind of agree with her. Sometimes I feel out of place because of my clothes. If everyone else dressed up…"

"You'd just blend in. And you're not a blending in kind of person."

Before Jennifer could respond, Pearl yelled from the front of a gift shop. "Look at all this stuff. You can even buy hooch."

"Lookie here," George shouted from a cocktail lounge across the way, trying to get Pearl's attention. "They got a gin mill right here in the open."

Pearl squealed and hurried over to him. "Can you believe it? So many kinds of booze. April, you gonna stop for a snort?"

"It's a little early for that, Pearl. Besides, if we really want a drink, we can get one on the airplane."

Her eyes widened. "You can?" She hurried over to George, no doubt to tell him.

"While they're busy, let's make a break for it," I said to Jennifer. With any luck, we could board the plane without them.

As we hurried to the gate, I almost asked if Jennifer was nervous about flying, but I stopped myself from putting that idea in her head. Instead, I asked, "Are you excited?"

"Yes!" she answered with a tight smile.

"Could we get lucky enough for George and

Pearl to miss the flight?" It was half an hour until boarding time, but I still held out hope for a quiet, ghost-free experience.

A loud whooping sound came from behind us. I grabbed Jennifer by the arm and pulled her behind a planter filled with huge ferns as George and Pearl passed us. The employee driving the courtesy cart, and his two elderly passengers were oblivious to the two ghosts hanging on the back. They squealed like they were on an amusement park ride.

George craned his neck to ogle a female flight attendant. Pearl gave him a shove and he fell off the cart. Pearl hopped off, tripped, and landed on top of him. Her apology lacked the slightest touch of sincerity.

Someone poked me in the arm. A security guard peered down at us.

"What are you two doing?" he asked suspiciously.

I forced a laugh. "Oh, just playing a little game with our friends."

"The airport is no place for games."

"Yes, sir," I said, wishing he could tell that to George and Pearl.

An announcement came over the loudspeaker.

"That's us." I stood and motioned for Jennifer to follow me. We joined the long line at the gate, boarded, and soon found our seats in row fourteen.

I motioned for her take the window seat.

"Are you sure?" She looked at my ticket and at

the seat numbers. I'd reserved the aisle seat for myself. "Who's sitting in the middle seat?"

"Hopefully no one. If someone claims the seat, I'll offer to switch with them so we can still sit together." I had my fingers crossed that the flight wasn't full.

We stowed our suitcases in the overhead compartment, then got settled into our seats.

I pulled out a small notebook that I'd been using to plan our trip. "I don't like to plan every moment, but if there's anything you don't want to miss out on, let me know. As long as we get lots of good New Orleans food, I won't complain. But there must be a museum or two you want to check out."

Jennifer grinned. "I had hoped we could go to the Museum of Art. They're having a costume and textile exhibit."

"We'll definitely have to make time for that." I'd make sure of it. "There's a Southern Food and Beverage Museum that might be fun to check out, but it's kind of off the beaten track. Besides, I think I'd rather consume the food and drink instead of learning about it. I've already had an expert teach me about Louisiana cooking." A memory of Chef Emile Toussaint stabbed me in the gut. And here I thought I'd stopped missing him. Jennifer must have sensed my momentary sadness.

"I wish I could have met him."

"Me, too." I pictured Chef watching me from the corner of the kitchen as he sipped a glass of wine. "He was special."

A woman wearing an off-white cloche hat, and a fur stole draped around her shoulders headed towards us. Perhaps I was in denial because it took a few seconds for me to recognize her.

"Oh, good," Pearl said, her voice grating on my nerves. "You saved me a seat. But what about George?"

"What are you doing here?" I whispered.

"What am I what?" Jennifer must have seen the annoyance written all over my face. Her eyes widened. "Oh. They made it on the plane, didn't they?"

"Shh…" I didn't want to get thrown off the plane, and my fellow travelers might not like the idea of me talking to ghosts during their flight. I took the journal out of my backpack and wrote, "Pearl is here, but I don't see George." I suspected he was checking out the flight attendants.

Pearl climbed over me and got comfortable in the seat between us. I motioned to Jennifer so she wouldn't put anything on the seat. Any solid objects would go right through Pearl, but she might take it as an insult. I hoped no living person showed up to claim the seat. I didn't want to have to pretend not to listen to her rant and rave about the rudeness of others.

As we waited for take-off, Pearl regaled me with stories of her days in New Orleans, and I repeated the highlights to Jennifer.

"Prohibition had passed before I arrived, but it was a few months before anything changed. I got a job at a classy dance hall making a nickel a dance. It was pretty good money at the time, and I was very popular." She wiggled her eyebrows for emphasis.

"I'm sure you were."

As I took a closer look at the fur draped around Pearl's shoulders, I sucked in a breath.

"What's wrong?" Jennifer asked.

"Pearl's fur stole is staring at me. It has a head, and I think I see teeth."

Jennifer began to giggle. "It sounds like a fox stole. I know they're kinda creepy, but they used to be all the rage. I found one at a vintage shop and almost bought it, but I couldn't do it."

Pearl's mouth turned into a pout, and she stroked the fur. "Did she call my beautiful stole creepy? I'll have you know this is a genuine Russian fox scarf worth twenty-five dollars!"

"That cost twenty-five dollars?" I repeated for Jennifer's benefit. "I guess that was a lot of money back in those days."

"Probably three or four hundred." Jennifer stared at the spot where Pearl sat. "I wish I could see her. She sounds very stylish."

Pearl batted her eyelashes at Jennifer. "Thanks. You're a peach."

I wasn't at all sure what she meant, but I told Jennifer, "She called you a peach."

Jennifer grinned. "Really? Thank you, Pearl. That means a lot coming from you. There's something I've been wondering."

"What's that?"

"When you describe Pearl, it seems like she changes her outfits. Can ghosts wear whatever they want?"

I imagined Jennifer considering the afterlife might not be so bad if you had an unlimited selection of clothes to wear.

"Well, I just…" Pearl began, then cocked her head. "I don't really know where I get my clothes. I remember an outfit I wore and then I'm wearing it."

I repeated Pearl's explanation to Jennifer who got a dreamy look on her face. "That must be wonderful."

The engines began to roar, and I leaned back in my seat. Maybe it wouldn't be a problem having Pearl and George along after all.

No sooner had I leaned back in my seat and closed my eyes, then Pearl let out a shriek.

"What is he doing?" She climbed over me, which wasn't really necessary since she could have gone through me, but I appreciated it.

The "he" of course was George, and what George was doing was trying to kiss a real, live flight attendant who twitched every time his lips came close to her cheek.

"Looks like George is in trouble." I gave Jennifer a play by play of the fit Pearl was throwing. After I got tired of listening to her scolding George, I dug in my bag for my headphones.

Jennifer flipped through the pages of the in-flight magazine. "You must have had an interesting life surrounded by ghosts."

"Chef Emile was the first ghost I ever saw. I thought he was a hallucination. It took me a while to accept that my imagination wasn't playing tricks on me."

"But now you see other ghosts too. Do you ever wonder why?"

It wasn't the first time I'd pondered that question, but I'd never learned the answer. "I don't see all ghosts, thank goodness. I have no idea why I see the ones I do. I mean, Dalton came to me like some sort of ghostly referral, but I don't know about the others."

"But you never saw any ghosts before Chef? Not even when you were little?"

"Nope."

"Maybe you saw things that you didn't understand at the time." Jennifer said. "When we're children, we sometimes take things for granted."

"My childhood was chaotic, as you know." I'd told her about how much my mother struggled as a free spirit raising two children on her own with little support. "That's probably why I had an imaginary friend. Her name was Fannie, and she wore this lovely white nightgown with her hair in braids. She taught me how to play whist. My mother loved Fanny, because she kept me occupied for hours. She used to call her my babysitter."

Jennifer tilted her head. "Your imaginary friend

taught you to play a Victorian card game? How is that even possible?"

I chuckled. "It does sound sort of silly, doesn't it? I'm sure I'd learned it somewhere."

"What happened to Fanny? Did you just stop seeing her?"

It was so long ago, I tried to remember. "I was only five or six years old at the time. Fanny told me that she'd been in love with a man who lived in our town, but her parents didn't approve. They sent her away, but she promised she would come back and marry him."

"Wow. You really had quite an imagination when you were little. I'm surprised you didn't end up writing romance novels. So did she come back and marry him?"

"No…" The memories came flooding back. "She told me she'd died from the flu I think."

"That's sad." Jennifer leaned closer. "You know that imaginary friends aren't usually dead."

"What? I, well…" I had never considered that Fanny might have been a ghost. "My mother always called her my imaginary playmate. I never thought to question it, except that…"

"Except what?" Jennifer waved me to continue.

"One day, we were at a diner, and I, of course, made my mom get a table big enough so Fanny could sit with us. Mom wouldn't let me order food for Fanny, but I'd always ask for an extra plate so I could share mine. And then…" I pictured myself walking up to an older man in the diner and telling him Fannie had a message for him. Did that really happen?

"And then, what?" Jennifer asked, fully engrossed in my story.

"I told a man—a complete stranger—that Fanny loved him but died before she could come back and marry him. His eyes got as wide as saucers, and he stared at me for what felt like a very long time. Then he reached out and took my hand and said, 'Thank you.' The woman who was with him freaked out and started screaming at me, calling me a witch. My mother grabbed me by the arm and dragged me out of there."

Jennifer gave me a few moments to process my memories before asking for the rest of the story.

A tear slipped down my cheek. "I never saw Fanny again. I thought I'd done something wrong and chased her away." I dug in my backpack for a tissue to wipe my eyes.

"Maybe you did something right," Jennifer said. "Don't you see? Fanny was a ghost, and she couldn't move on until the man she loved knew she hadn't betrayed him."

"You think so?"

She nodded. "Yes, I do. And would you please pass me one of those tissues?"

CHAPTER 5

The rest of the flight was uneventful except for Pearl stopping by every so often to rant or rave about the other passengers.

"Why aren't you sitting up front?" she asked. "The seats are much bigger and they're pouring champagne like it's cheap gin."

I explained first class to her, including the comparable pricing.

"You'd think they could afford nicer duds. There is one gal I'm pretty sure is wearing cashmere. I had a cashmere sweater once. It was the bee's knees, soft as a baby kitten."

I closed my eyes, hoping she'd get my hint and go bother someone else. But since I was the only one who could hear her, she kept chatting. When the pilot announced we were about to land, I let out a sigh of relief.

As soon as we ditched George and Pearl, which I

hoped would be easy in New Orleans, I could look forward to a delightful vacation.

Five days and four nights of sightseeing, shopping, and wonderful food in the French Quarter with no ghosts to bother me.

THE TAXI'S WIPERS BEAT A SLOW RHYTHM AS WE MADE our way through the city on our way to the French Quarter.

I stared out the window at the gray skies and sighed. "I was afraid we might get rain."

Jennifer wasn't about to let a little precipitation get her down. "You know how people in Arizona say, 'it's a dry heat'? Well, this is a warm wet. It's not like back home where it only rains when it's cold. I don't mind getting a little wet."

"Neither do I." I only wish I'd thought twice about my footwear choice. Were sandals going to cut it in the rain?

As we got out of the taxi, I got my answer when my foot slipped on the stone sidewalk. "Thank goodness I brought sneakers." They weren't as stylish, but at least I wouldn't break a hip in them.

The lobby of the Hotel Monteleone was old school elegance, from the crystal chandeliers to the enormous grandfather clock. On the right a sign said, "Carousel Bar." We'd have to check out that famous landmark later.

The desk clerk slid two key envelopes across the

counter. "Your rooms are on the fourteenth floor." He waited as if making sure I approved.

"With a view, right?"

He brightened. "They have the best view possible. If there's anything you need, please don't hesitate to ask. The carousel bar opens at 5:30, but you'll want to get there early if you'd like to sit at the bar. There's usually a wait."

"I think we'll go explore the area after we freshen up." A bell hop appeared to take our bags, but I waved him off, preferring to wheel my own bag to the room.

When we stepped inside the elevator, I pressed the button for the fourteenth floor.

Jennifer stared at the buttons. "There's no thirteen. It goes from twelve to fourteen."

"No one would want to stay on the thirteenth floor. Too many people think the number is bad luck."

"But then that means the fourteenth floor is really the thirteenth."

"Oh, right." I remember the desk clerk's expression when he told us we were on the fourteenth floor. Were people really that suspicious?

Jennifer cocked her head to one side. "So why does it matter?"

"Good thing we're not afraid of no ghosts," I joked.

Jennifer eyes widened. "Are you saying this hotel is haunted?"

"Practically every hotel in the French Quarter

claims to be haunted, but it's all in fun. If people knew what ghosts were really like, they'd be less excited about having them around. They're less scary than I always thought they'd be, but also less exciting."

"But you've never met an evil ghost, have you?" Jennifer asked as we stepped from the elevator. She rubbed her arms. "Brr. They sure have the AC cranked up. I'm glad I brought a sweater along."

A sense of foreboding followed me as we walked to the end of the hallway, but I brushed it off. I tapped the key against my door, and when it beeped and blinked green, I pushed it open. "Want to check out my room first?"

"Sure." Jennifer followed me into a luxurious room with high ceilings decorated in soft pastels.

Setting my suitcase by the closet, I threw open the curtains, pleased to see that the view I'd been promised didn't disappoint. A few blocks away, past low buildings, a wide river curved around the city. "That's the Mississippi River right out there."

Jennifer hurried over to look. "Wow. The mighty Mississippi. Did you know that the Algonquin Indians gave it that name? It means Great River."

"You are always full of information, Jennifer."

"Sorry," she said shyly. "I've been researching New Orleans ever since you said we were coming here. I can't wait to see everything."

"I can't wait to taste everything." After a quick check of the time, I suggested we freshen up, then go explore the French Quarter. "I'm planning to stay on West Coast time since we're only here for four nights. I'm hoping it will help with the jet lag, although knowing you, you'll probably be up with the sun."

Thirty minutes later, we stepped onto Royal Street and spotted Pearl and George walking arm in arm heading our way. Pearl held a tall glass with a pink and orange liquid that sloshed over the side. I was about to tell her that glass wasn't allowed on the street, but then I remembered that the drink was as ghostly as she was.

"They're here," I whispered to Jennifer. "And I think Pearl is already a bit tipsy."

Pearl either hadn't heard my comment or ignored it. "If I'd known that the scene was so lively here, I would have found a way to get here years ago. When you're dead, no one can arrest you, shoot you, or stab you. The worst they can do is insult you, and I've had gobs of time to work on my comebacks."

"That's great, Pearl," I said. "Have fun. Looks like you don't need to hang around us."

Pearl's smile faded as she realized she was being dismissed. A tiny pang stabbed at me for being rude to her for no reason, but she'd get over her disappointment. Besides, I'd been clear as I could be that I didn't want her to come along.

It seemed that the antique shops in the French Quarter had all closed for the day just as the restaurants and bars came to life. Loud music of all types spilled into the streets.

Jennifer pressed her face up against the window of Royal Antiques. "Look at all the beautiful chandeliers."

"We have enough chandeliers," I said, not wanting to be tempted.

She gave me a mischievous smile. "Are you sure?"

"Pretty sure." I checked the map on my phone. "Let's head for the French Market. It's several blocks of shops and food vendors. Last time I was here, you could get a great po' boy or muffuletta."

"A what or a what?"

I laughed. "They're both sandwiches but very different from each other. A po' boy is usually fried shrimp or crawfish on a French roll and a muffuletta is Italian cold cuts on a round roll. The food here is incredibly diverse. And there's plenty of other things to eat if you're not in the mood for a sandwich."

We strolled along Royal Street, then turned down Pirates Alley, a narrow passage said to be haunted. I held my breath, but exhaled in relief when we only encountered living, breathing people.

The alley let out onto a large square.

"I know where we are." Jennifer could hardly hide her excitement. "This is Jackson Square. And that means that that—" She pointed to her left. "That is St. Louis Cathedral. It's stunning."

The Square was known for being surrounded by artists and performers, but they must have stayed away due to the rain. A lone saxophonist crooned a jazz ballad.

As we made our way around the square, Jennifer asked, "What's a beg net?"

Following her gaze, I spotted Café du Monde. "Oh, you must mean beignet."

"It's pronounced ben-yay?" She covered her mouth with her hand. "I'm glad you're the only one who heard me."

We turned down Decatur Street, the liveliest part of the quarter yet. By the time we made it past the restaurants and souvenir shops, I was famished and beginning to question my decision.

"Is it much further?" Jennifer asked.

"It didn't look this far on the map."

Just as I was about to suggest stopping into one of the many restaurants we passed, I spotted the sign for the French Market. We made our way through the arch and into a covered marketplace with stalls selling crafts, souvenirs, and food.

Jennifer stopped in front of a spice emporium and pointed at a sign. "Gator on a stick?"

"No, thank you." I spotted another sign. "How about splitting a shrimp po' boy? Then we can go to Café du Monde for beignets afterwards."

She grinned. "You mean beg nets?"

THE NEXT MORNING, I WAS AWAKENED BY A WOMAN'S grating voice. *Pearl.*

"There you are," she cooed, as if we were long lost friends. "I've been hunting all over this hotel for you. You can only imagine what I've seen. Some people should take their showers with their clothes on, if you know what I mean."

I sleepily rubbed my eyes. "What are you doing here bothering me at this time of the morning?"

"Watcha talkin' about?" She strutted to the window and reached for the curtains as if to pull them back, but she hadn't mastered moving things in the real world, thank goodness. Turning back to me, she put one hand on her hip. "The sun's been up for at least an hour or two."

A glance at the bedside clock told me it was eight a.m. "I had planned to sleep in today. It's only six o'clock California time."

"Yeah, well you ain't in California. Besides, I got someone for you to meet."

"No, no, no," I protested to no avail.

"C'mon in, guys." Pearl waved her arms inviting someone into my room. "She's decent."

"I'm in my pajamas." Which meant I was technically decent, sure, but not exactly dressed to entertain a guest. "Can you let me—"

Before I finished my sentence, George appeared. "She's gonna need to open the door."

"What are you talking about?" I didn't like anyone, even a ghost, ordering me around. "I don't need to do anything, for your information."

"Will you just open the door, sweetie?" Pearl asked in a sing-song voice. "Please?"

I sighed, then went to the door, flipped the deadbolt but left the chain attached and peered through the gap. In the hall stood a middle-aged, black man with curly hair, thinning on the top, wearing… was that a smoking jacket?

"You need to invite him in." Pearl said.

"Why? Is he a vampire?" He didn't look like one, but it seemed prudent to ask.

Pearl huffed. She leaned over my shoulder and told the man, "Don't mind her. Come on in."

I pulled the door open wider and stepped back. The fact that he could hear and see Pearl only meant one thing.

My visitor was a ghost.

CHAPTER 6

I took in Pearl's eagerness and the slumped shoulders of the guy in the smoking jacket and came to a conclusion. "I'm not interested in solving anyone's murder. I'm on vacation, remember?"

"But April…"

"We're only here for four nights. That means just three full days to tour the city, see the sights, and eat my weight in southern food. Our schedule is packed tight with no time to spare. Besides, if his death has gone unsolved this long, then it can wait for someone else to be the hero. I'm sorry, Mr. …"

"Cedric LeBlanc, ma'am." The ghost reached out a hand, but I knew mine would go right through his, so I didn't bother to try to shake it.

"When did you die?"

He gave an exaggerated shiver. "I don't like the sound of that. Am I really dead?"

"I'm afraid so, Mr. LeBlanc."

"I'd rather you called me Cedric, ma'am." He sighed. "The details are a bit hazy, mind you, but the last thing I remember it was the middle of the night."

"What night?"

"Last night."

Spirits often lost track of time after they left their bodies. Not surprising, when you thought about it. Dying had to be very disorienting. "What date was 'last night'?"

"Let's see." He scratched his chin. "It was Monday night, September eighth. No, Monday was the ninth, wasn't it?"

"Today's the tenth." Was I looking at a brand-new ghost? "You're saying you've only been dead a few hours?"

"That's right," Pearl chimed in. "His body's probably laying right where it fell. He lives alone, so it might be weeks before someone missed him. Seems like at least someone should call the police, so they know there's been a murder."

Before I could ask why Pearl was so sure Cedric had been murdered, someone tapped lightly on the door. After checking through the peephole, I let Jennifer in.

She looked fresh and perky, as usual, in a flow-ered sundress and ballet flats. "I thought I heard you talking. Did Pearl and George come back?"

"And they brought a friend. Let me get dressed and I'll tell you everything."

"It's beautiful outside. Sunny and not too hot."

Grateful for a break from the rain, I pulled a sundress off its hanger where I'd hung it the night before. Most of the wrinkles had fallen out, so I took it into the bathroom to change in private. Staring at my face in the mirror, I asked myself, "How did this become my life?" Was I destined to spend the rest of my days solving murders for ghosts who had no one else to go to?

I splashed cold water on my face, dragged my brush through my hair, and got dressed. The sooner we checked out Cedric LeBlanc's home, the sooner we could continue enjoying our vacation.

WE LEFT THE AIR-CONDITIONED COMFORT OF THE hotel and stepped onto Royal Street. It was only mid-morning, and it was already warm, but at least it wasn't raining. The French Quarter, buzzing the night before, was now nearly deserted. Cedric had assured us it was a short walk up Royal Street to the streetcar, so I let him lead the way. Jennifer's eyes lit up when we passed the QT Pie Boutique until she saw the lingerie in the window, probably too embarrassed to look in front of me, her much older boss. Good thing she couldn't see or hear Pearl.

"Oh, honey." Pearl gushed as she pressed her face against the window for a better look. "That feathered number would be perfect for you." She seemed to get miffed at being ignored until I reminded her that Jennifer couldn't see ghosts.

Pearl skipped ahead as Jennifer asked, "What did she say?"

George distracted me by ogling her, and I scolded him. "Get away from her, George, or I'll get Pearl to keep you in line."

"What?" he protested. "I wasn't doin' nothin'."

None of the antique shops or boutiques were open this early, but I kept an eye out for a coffee shop. We were crossing Canal Street, which Cedric explained was the border between the Quarter and the Central Business District, when I spotted French Truck Coffee.

"We'll be right back," I told the three ghosts, leaving them behind on the sidewalk as I ducked inside. The aroma of freshly ground beans filled the small space. I ordered a café au lait and turned to ask Jennifer for her order.

She held a tea menu. "Look at all their teas. They have Versailles Earl Grey with lavender and corn-flower petals."

"That sounds lovely."

"And they have Southern Black tea. I wonder what that's like."

"Probably sweet, since that's the default for tea when you're in the South. Which do you want?" I asked impatiently, not wanting to keep the barista waiting.

"Cappuccino, please."

"You are a creature of habit, aren't you?"

"Oh." Jennifer's face fell. "Should I order some-thing else?"

"There's absolutely nothing wrong with knowing what you like. Don't let anyone tell you differently."

While we waited for our drinks, Jennifer asked, "What does Cedric look like?"

"Sometimes I forget you can't see the ghosts. They seem so real to me. I mean, they are real, but it's hard to grasp that other people can't see them. Let's see. Cedric is medium height, not thin but not fat, with brown skin and short curly hair that's thinning on top."

"That's not much of a description."

I closed my eyes and pictured his face. "He has sort of a round face with chubby cheeks and twinkling eyes that crinkle up when he smiles. Come to think of it, he seems to smile a lot considering his very recent death."

"How old is, um, was he?"

"I'd say around fifty or maybe mid-fifties."

As we stepped back outside with our coffees, I happened to notice the street sign. "I thought we were on Royal Street."

"All the streets change when you leave the French Quarter," Cedric explained. "Royal Street changes to St. Charles. We get the streetcar at the next corner." He led the way as he called out over his shoulder. "Should be along any minute now."

Jennifer was unusually excited at the prospect of riding on a streetcar. "Did you know the St. Charles streetcar line has been operating since 1835? It's the oldest continuously operating streetcar line in the world, and it's even on the National Register of Historic Places."

"I didn't know that." Vacationing with Jennifer was like bringing along your own personal tour guide. To make sure she knew I appreciated her commentary, I added, "Thanks for sharing."

A green antique-looking streetcar soon arrived, and we climbed on board. I bought us two three-day Jazzy passes. One perk of being a ghost? Free admission pretty much everywhere.

The streetcar was half-full, with most of the riders appearing to be on their way to work. Maybe the other tourists were sensible enough to sleep in late. Jennifer and I found a seat on a wooden bench toward the back and Cedric sat across the aisle.

Pearl stayed standing, one hand holding onto a bar. "I swear I rode this exact same streetcar the last time I was in town."

"So, Cedric…" I kept my voice low. I had a few questions for the ghost but didn't want to be over-heard by other riders. "Tell me what happened last night, before… you know."

"Before I died?" He grimaced at the word. "Still can hardly believe it."

"What do you remember?"

He stared off into space for a long moment. "It's fuzzy. Why is it fuzzy?"

"It's not uncommon. I'm not sure why, but other ghosts have told me they can't remember what happened during the minutes or sometimes hours before their death. Sometimes the memories come back, but often they don't. They might not have needed help solving their murders if they remembered everything that happened. Well, unless a stranger attacked them from behind."

"It's hardly ever a stranger, though, is it?" Jennifer whispered.

I shook my head, but didn't want to tell Cedric just yet that he probably knew the person who killed him. It was an unsettling thought.

"Think back to yesterday," I suggested. "What *do* you remember?"

Cedric's brow furrowed. "I was at Pete's."

"Is Pete a friend of yours?"

A smile played on his lips. "Pete's Pit Stop. It's a local bar."

"Oh, got it. Do you remember who else was there?"

"Sure, at least the regulars. Jimmy Joe and Maurice and a few other guys. Mighta been a few tourists. They wander in from time to time, but they don't usually hang around for long. It's not that kind of a place, ya know?

"Anything out of the ordinary happen while you were there?"

He took a moment, then answered, "Nah. Bill put the Saints game on, and the bar got too loud, so I went home. I watched the rest of the game at home."

"Who's Bill?"

"The bartender. Good guy."

I'd wait and make my own decision about who

was a good guy if it came to that. "So, after you got home, what do you remember?"

"Had a beer." He paused to think some more. "Watched the rest of the game."

I glanced at Jennifer who watched me expectantly and shrugged. "Not a lot to go on so far."

"Oh." Cedric perked up. "Jimmy Joe came by."

"Your buddy from the bar?" I asked. "What did he want?"

"Nothin' much. Just hung out for a bit. Had a beer." His face relaxed as if enjoying the comforting memory, then a cloud seemed to cross his face. "Then he left."

"That's it? Did you two fight?"

"Fight? Me and Jimmy Joe never fight. He'd do anything for me. Like if I needed a kidney, I bet he'd give me his. I know he could have one of mine. Oh." He frowned. "If I was, ya know…"

No reason to dwell on that thought. "What happened after Jimmy Joe left?"

He scratched his head. "Can't remember anything after that."

Jennifer stared out the window as we skirted the border of the Garden District. Majestic old mansions lined each side of the street.

Cedric jumped up and reached for the pull cord, but his hand went through it.

I gave him a shrug and pulled the cord myself. "Looks like our stop is next," I told Jennifer.

When the streetcar came to a stop, Jennifer and I

made our way to the rear exit, followed by the three ghosts.

Pearl kept up a running monologue, as usual. "I swear, I believe I may have ridden this very streetcar the last time I visited New Orleans."

"You already said that," I muttered, but she either didn't hear me or didn't care.

We found ourselves at a nondescript intersection. Napoleon Street had a wide grassy median like St. Charles Avenue.

"Used to be a streetcar ran up and down Napoleon, too," Cedric said. "That was before I was born."

Pearl turned to him and asked, "You lived your whole life in this town?"

"Tenth generation," he said proudly.

We followed him north on Napoleon past small houses and apartments. The wide median and huge, old oak trees gave the street a timeless feel. When we passed by a school, the trees bordering the street had been cut down.

I stepped closer to one of the stumps that had once been a magnificent tree. "That's sad."

Cedric shrugged. "Woulda been sadder if a limb had fallen on some kid. Thing is, with the hurricanes and the storms, we lose a lot of trees every year."

Pearl piped up. "Well, I for one think that's a crying shame. N'Awlins wouldn't look the same without all the majestic oaks."

Cedric stopped and scowled at Pearl. "It's not

N'Awlins. And it ain't New *Orleeens* neither, ya know?"

Pearl ignored him, walking in front of the group. George lagged a few steps behind her, and I suspected it was so he could watch her swinging her hips with every step.

I was about to ask how much farther it was when Cedric pointed ahead. "That's my house right up there."

Pearl arrived first and stood on the sidewalk facing the little cottage. "Well, ain't that the cutest little bungalow? All it needs is a coat of paint and a few rose bushes out front, and it would be just darlin'." She'd picked up a southern accent which seemed to get stronger by the minute.

I shared Pearl's thoughts with Jennifer, who said under her breath, "It's a little late to be giving Cedric home decorating tips. Anyway, I like it just the way it is."

"Do you know if the door is unlocked?" I asked Cedric as we caught up to him.

"If it ain't, I can show you where I hid an extra key to the back door."

"I think I'll knock first, in case the neighbors are watching." I climbed the cement steps to a small porch. "By the way, what's our story in case someone asks why I'm looking for you?"

I waited for Cedric to offer a suggestion, but Jennifer spoke up first.

"We can say that I'm Cedric's long-lost daughter."

I looked from Jennifer to Cedric and back to Jennifer. "Sure, that might work. Except he's black."

"Oh. I suppose that won't work then." Jennifer quickly recovered. "His adopted daughter?"

"Or my ex-girlfriend," Cedric said. "Although I'm not sure how to explain her Yankee accent."

Pearl muttered, "She's a little young for you, sport."

"Maybe you and I met online, and you offered to show us around town." I thought that might work, and since no one had a better idea, that's what we went with.

I rang the doorbell, then knocked. I twisted the doorknob just in case it had been left unlocked, but it didn't turn. Cedric led the way around to the back.

"The door's ajar." I hesitated, then turned to the three ghosts looking over my shoulder. "Will one of you go in and make sure no one's in there? No one alive, that is?"

"I'll do it." George walked through the door, returning about a minute later. "Okay. Coast is clear."

I sucked in a breath and pushed the door wider, not sure what to expect. We stepped into a hallway. The first door on the right opened into a bedroom, and on the left was a laundry room.

"Are you sure you want to see this?" George asked. At first, I thought he was talking to me, but then I saw his eyes were fixed on Cedric. "It ain't easy to see yourself just lying there, especially when you didn't see it coming."

Cedric nodded. "Let's go."

George motioned for us to follow him down the hall. "In the living room."

I sucked in a breath at the sight of Cedric's lifeless body on the floor.

CHAPTER 7

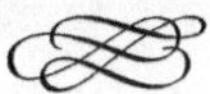

$\mathcal{I}$ should have been ready to see Cedric's body, but after meeting him as a walking, talking ghost, it came as something of a shock. He lay on his back, arms wide, palms up, as if he were resting, a statue about eight inches tall on the floor nearby. An end table had been knocked over, but everything else appeared to be in its place.

"You okay, buddy?" George asked, placing a hand on the other ghost's shoulder.

Cedric stared, not saying a word, then knelt down next to his body. "I guess I really am dead." He turned to look up at us. "Hadn't really sunk in until right this moment."

Knowing that Cedric had been dead for hours, I didn't need to hurry. Still, the police needed to be called so they could start solving his murder. Crouching next to him, I went through the motions of checking for a pulse. I touched his wrist, and the cool skin made a shiver go down my spine.

Under his head, a spot of dark red looked like dried blood and confirmed in my mind he'd been hit from behind with a heavy object, probably the statue.

Jennifer glanced into the bedroom. "The mattress looks askew. I wonder if someone was looking for money. Do people really keep cash there?"

"I did," Cedric said. "What's so wrong about that?"

"How much?" I asked.

"How should I know?" Jennifer answered.

"Sorry, I was asking Cedric. Where'd he go?" I asked, before spotting him in the bedroom.

I stood back up and pulled out my phone, thinking of what to say on the call. How much emotion should I show for this man that I'd supposedly had some sort of online relationship with? I'd just have to wing it.

The dispatcher answered the call and asked me to state my emergency.

Doing my best to sound upset and somewhat panicked, I said, "I just found my friend." I paused briefly. "He's lying on his living room floor."

"What's his condition?"

Closing my eyes, I imagined what I would feel if I'd just found the body of someone I knew. "I think he's… dead." After a deep breath in and out, I added, "I'm sure he's dead."

The woman on the other end of the phone went into action. "Have you checked his pulse?"

"There's no pulse. No breathing. And he feels… cold." As I said the words, a rush of sympathy washed over me for Cedric.

"We're sending someone right away. What's your location?"

"It's on Liberty Street." I gave Cedric a questioning look and he told me the street number which I repeated over the phone.

"And your friend's name?"

"Cedric." I held my hand over the speaker and whispered to the ghost. "What's your last name again?"

"LeBlanc."

"His name is Cedric LeBlanc," I told the dispatcher.

"We're sending the paramedics and the police." She continued asking questions about his condition until I'd convinced her he was truly dead.

"Where's my talisman?" Cedric cried out suddenly.

"What?" I asked, forgetting I was still on the phone.

"What is it?" the dispatcher asked. "Do you want me to stay on the phone with you until someone arrives?"

"Thank you, but I have a friend with me." Besides, I had a few more questions for Cedric before the police arrived.

Cedric, however, was in no mood for a conversation. "Someone stole my talisman. That musta been why they murdered me."

"A talisman?" I asked, pulling Freddie's pendant from under my shirt and holding it out to show him. "Like this one?"

He looked at it more closely. "Kinda like yours, but different, ya know?"

Jennifer tapped my arm. "We might want to get our stories straight before the authorities arrive."

"If we can come up with a reason we connected, like something we had in common, then—"

Cedric interrupted me. "But, my talisman…"

"Yes, we'll get to that later, I promise. What hobbies do you have?"

"Hobbies?" He stared at me with his brows drawn together.

"Yes, hobbies. You know, those things you do when you're not working or sleeping?"

"I like to watch football."

I held back from saying I didn't think watching sports on TV qualified as a hobby. Who was I to judge? "What do you do on the weekends or in the evening, when there aren't any football games on? Or any sports to watch, for that matter."

He nodded as if understanding. "There's a bar not far from here."

"Your hobby is going to a bar?" A note of disapproval might have slipped into my voice.

"You don't get it. I go, have a couple of beers, see my buddies, and hang out." He must have sensed my skepticism, because he kept explaining. "Look, I live alone. Took early retirement. Got no children. My sister moved away. Going to Pete's Pit

Stop is my social life. I'm a people person, not some introverted loner."

There wasn't much point in telling a ghost there was more to life than sports and beer, and we still needed a cover story to explain my presence at his house. I walked over to a tall bookcase, overflowing with books. At least he liked to read.

Two entire shelves were devoted to cookbooks.

"You bake?" I asked.

He grinned. "Best pecan pie this side of the Rocky Mountains."

Now we were getting somewhere. "I love to bake, too. I'm always looking for new recipes. What's your favorite recipe for—" Sirens interrupted me.

Jennifer hurried to the window and peeked through the curtains. "There's an ambulance pulling in the driveway. And a police car right behind it."

I unlocked the front door and stepped onto the porch. Cedric joined me.

"Stay close by in case I need you to help convince the police I knew you."

He chuckled. "I ain't got nowhere to go."

CHAPTER 8

etective Earl Bowman, a sandy-haired, relatively trim forty-ish man with caterpillar eyebrows and a snug-fitting uniform, asked Jennifer and me to wait for him while he and his younger partner conducted their preliminary investigation.

Bowman spoke briefly with the paramedics, then gave Cedric's body a quick scan and checked his pockets. There wasn't much to find other than some spare change and a wallet, which he bagged.

After the body was carried away on a stretcher, Bowman got our names and contact information, then began his questioning. His partner, a younger, slimmer, taller man, stayed close, but didn't say a word. "I believe you mentioned you'd never met Cedric LeBlanc before you found his body this morning?"

"Not in person." I gave him my story about how he'd offered to show my assistant and me around

New Orleans, but didn't answer the door when we arrived. "The front door was locked, so we went around the back. When I saw the door was ajar, I got worried. I only wish I'd gotten here earlier."

He shook his head. "Unless you were here around midnight, it wouldn't have made a difference."

After making a mental note of the time of death, I asked, "Do you think it was a burglar? He told me he always wore a talisman, kind of a pendant, for good luck. But he wasn't wearing it when I… when he was… lying there."

The officer narrowed his eyes. "Looked like natural causes to me. Do you have a reason to think different?"

"Natural causes?" I glanced over at Cedric who scowled and shook his head. Turning back to the officer, I said, "I saw the statue lying on the ground nearby, so I figured someone had hit him over the head with it."

"Probably knocked it over when he collapsed." The officer shrugged. "Did you see the guy? Doubt if he exercised much. Pretty much lived on beer and boudin balls from the looks of him."

"He did like his beer," I agreed, though I had no idea what a boudin ball might be. Still, unless it was some kind of bowling ball, I doubted that was what had killed him.

"Looked to me like he fell backwards and hit his head on the edge of the table. Probably knocked the statue over at the same time."

At least I knew that the coroner or medical examiner wouldn't be so quick to jump to conclusions. Any time there was a sudden death, an investigation had to be done, no matter how much it might appear to be natural causes.

Before I could ask any more questions, a plump woman around my age burst through the front door, her curly afro framing her head like a halo. "What's going on? Where's my brother?"

"Nadine!" Cedric greeted her and rushed up to her to give her a hug, but his arms went right through her. She shivered in reaction to his touch, just as I'd done whenever coming in contact with a ghost.

He watched as the officer led his sister to the sofa where he delivered the news.

She gasped. "No!" Tears began to stream down her face as she wailed, "It can't be. It can't be."

"Nadine, Nadine." Cedric helplessly watched her sobbing, then turned to me. "Do something."

I raised my eyebrows, hoping he'd understand it to mean, "Like what?" Looking around, I found a box of tissues which I handed to her. She took them from me without looking up.

Pearl's voice startled me, since I didn't realize she was still around. "Might get her a glass of water, girlie. That's the civilized thing to do in a situation like this."

Following her advice, I went into the kitchen and checked the refrigerator for bottled water. Unlike most bachelors I'd known, the refrigerator held butter, cream, eggs, and everything else a baker might need. As for drinks? Only beer. I found a clean glass in the dish drainer, hoping the local tap water was tolerable to drink.

When I returned, Nadine sobbed quietly into a handful of tissues as Bowman patted her shoulder. Someone must have told him that was the thing to do if someone was upset or grieving.

Nadine didn't seem to notice his gesture or much else through her tears, but after a little while, she wiped her face and sucked in a jagged breath. "I always knew he was on his way to an early grave if he didn't change his ways."

Bowman nodded. "We all think we're going to live forever, but if we don't take care—"

She grabbed the officer by the shoulder, interrupted him. "Tell me you'll find whoever did this."

Bowman's brows pulled together as his frown deepened. "Southern food was what did it. Too much butter and lard and not enough fresh fruits and vegetables. I should know. My cholesterol was through the roof until I changed my diet." His frown faded as he puffed out his chest proudly and patted his belly. "Doctors said I was on my way to an early grave until I lost forty pounds."

"So, it wasn't..." Nadine lowered her voice. "He wasn't murdered?"

The officer did his best to hide his smug expression, but I spotted it. "The coroner will take a look at him, but I expect he'll agree with me that the cause of death is due to cardiovascular causes. Hit his head on the table when he fell, but it doesn't look like that injury had anything to do with his death."

"You saying he had a heart attack?" Nadine huffed. "My brother had a ticker stronger than anyone. Everybody in our family lives to be a hundred or more. And besides—" She stopped mid-sentence as she finally noticed me hovering nearby. "Who are you?"

I handed her the glass of water. "I'm April, a friend of Cedric." When she didn't say anything, I kept talking. "I met him online. He was going to show my assistant and me around town. I'm so sorry about Cedric. This must be such a shock for you."

Nadine's gaze drifted from me to Jennifer then back to me. "Cedric never mentioned you."

Great. I figured the police would be the one's questioning my story, not his sister. "So, he tells you everything?"

"Hardly." She smirked. "It's just... and don't take this the wrong way, but you're not exactly his type."

The policeman stood and cleared his throat. "I can take you to see Cedric if you'd like."

She scrunched up her face as if she'd sucked on a lemon. "You mean his body? No thanks. I've gone my entire life never seeing a dead body, and I don't need to see one now. If you say he's dead, that's good enough for me."

The officer shifted his weight from foot to foot. "I see."

Nadine huffed. "I'm not sure you do see." She sounded just like a mother scolding her grown son and trying to talk some sense into him. "That body that they took outta here wasn't Cedric. When he died, his spirit left and went to meet our Heavenly Father, God willing. Although after the life he led, it could go either way." She paused as a dark cloud crossed her face. "What was left behind is just a shell—the vessel that God allowed him to inhabit while he wandered this earth, nothing more than that."

The officer nodded solemnly and handed her his card. "If you change your mind…"

I followed Bowman and his assistant to the door. "We're staying at the Hotel Monteleone through Friday if you want to get in touch with us. Or if you learn anything more."

Bowman handed me one of his cards, gave Jennifer a nod, and the two officers left.

"She looks so sad." Cedric sat down next to her in the spot Bowman had vacated. "Can't you tell her I'm here?"

Glancing over at Pearl, I raised my eyebrows, hoping she'd get the hint and explain things to him.

"Look, hon." Pearl threw an arm around his shoulder. "If April tells your sister she can see ghosts and in particular *your* ghost, she's gonna freak out. Or figure her for one of them charla…

charla… one of them fakers, you know? After all, your sis don't know April from Eve."

Cedric hung his head as the reality of his death began to sink in. He looked almost as forlorn as his sister. There wasn't much more we could do there, but before we left, I decided to ask Nadine about the talisman.

"Cedric said he wore it all the time, but I didn't see it when I found him."

Nadine scoffed. "That ridiculous, ugly thing? He said he wore it for luck. Didn't turn out to be too lucky for him, did it?"

I shook my head. "My first thought when I didn't see it anywhere was that he'd been killed for it. But Officer Bowman seems to think he died of natural causes."

Nadine's eyes widened. "You thought he'd been murdered, too?"

Oops. "I probably shouldn't have said that out loud."

Nadine's laugh startled me. "No wonder you two became friends. That's just the sort of thing Cedric woulda said. He loved those true crime shows."

"Yep." I gave her a little smile. "Crime and baking."

"Oh, you're a baker too? That's nice." She glanced over at the bookcase. "Maybe you'd like some of his cookbooks. I think collecting them was as much of a hobby for him as baking."

"That's very kind of you, but I don't think I'll

have any extra room in my suitcase after we get done shopping." I hated to leave her all alone in the empty house. "Is there anything we can do before we go? Anyone we can call?"

"Cedric was all the family I had." She pushed herself up from the sofa and carried her glass into the kitchen. When she returned, she said, "That was my first thought, too—that he was murdered. He hung around some unsavory characters."

"They weren't unsavory," Cedric said indignantly. "Just colorful. A whole lot more interesting than those church folk she hobnobs with."

Nadine gave me the once over. "Too bad he's dead. I think you two mighta been just right for each other." She sniffed. "Course anyone's better than that tramp Sally."

At the sound of that name, Cedric scowled. "Sally ain't a tramp. She's the prettiest little thing I ever did see."

"He didn't tell me much about her," I bluffed. "Except that she was pretty."

"Hah! That tells you about his taste in women." She sucked in a breath and let it out slowly. "I suppose she musta dumped him again. Maybe this time it stuck. Otherwise, he wouldn't have been going online looking for a new girlfriend. He was loyal that way."

I nodded as if I agreed. Handing her my card, I told her to call me if she needed anything. "I know we just met, but if there's anything we can do while we're in town, or if you need someone to talk to, that's my cell phone. Don't hesitate to call."

Before I knew it, Nadine wrapped me in a tight hug, rocking me from side to side like a rag doll before she released me. New tears had sprung up, but now there was a smile on her face.

"Thank you, April. I might just do that."

As I reached for the doorknob, the door swung open, nearly hitting me. A blonde women burst through the room and looked me in the eyes through thick, false eyelashes.

"Where's my Cedric?"

CHAPTER 9

Sally couldn't have been more than five feet tall, but her four-inch heels made her eye level with me. If her teased-up, bleached-blonde hair was any higher, she'd have to duck to get through the door.

Cedric appeared next to me wearing a huge grin. "Sally!"

Not sure what else to say, I sputtered, "Cedric's not here."

"Who are you?" Sally looked past me into the room and gestured to Nadine. "And what is she doing here? I got a call from one of the neighbors. He said there was an ambulance out front and a police car."

"Hello, Sally." Nadine said in a voice cold as ice. "That's April, Cedric's new girlfriend."

I'd read about eyes that "flashed with anger," but I'd never seen it until now. I could have sworn I saw flames in Sally's pupils.

"I'm not his new girlfriend." I gave Nadine a dirty look, but she just chuckled, enjoying the drama way too much.

Sally pushed past me into the room and stood with her hands on her hips. "Was the heck is going on here? What are you two up to?"

Nadine's smile evaporated. "Cedric is dead."

"Stop playing with me, Nadine. I know you never liked me, but telling me that Cedric is dead isn't going to make me go away."

Cedric hovered nearby, staring at her lovingly. "I always knew you loved me, Sally." He turned to me. "Nadine said she didn't, but I always knew your heart was true."

"Yeah, right," I mumbled.

"What?" Sally marched over to me. "If Nadine won't tell me where my sweetie-pie is, maybe you will."

"She's telling you the truth."

Pearl appeared next to me. "Cedric was right. She is a pretty little thing, even if it's hard to tell under all that makeup. If she blinks too fast, those false eyelashes might start a windstorm. And speaking of false…"

"I don't believe you." Sally took another step closer. "I don't believe either of you."

"They took him away," I blurted out.

"Took him away?" Sally swung around and glared at Nadine. "Where?"

Nadine handed Sally the card the officer had

given her. "Why don't you call Officer Bowman and find out."

"He's in jail?" She tore the card in half and tossed it on the ground. "That loser. If I never see him again it'll be too soon." She pointed a finger at me. "And you can tell him that the next time you see him."

"I don't need to tell him." I glanced over at Cedric. "I'm pretty sure he already knows."

"I bet he does." Sally spun around on her high heels and strutted out the door.

"Nice meeting you too," I said as she slammed the door behind her.

Nadine snickered. "Sorry." The snicker turned into a full laugh that she didn't seem to be able to stop. "Sorry. Sorry," she repeated with her mouth over her face.

Soon, her laughter turned into tears. "Cedric, you couyon."

Cedric hurried to her side. "I'm here, No-no. Imma stay with you. But why you gotta call me a *couyon*? I got as much sense as the next guy."

Nadine fell back onto the sofa and wailed. "Why'd you have to go and die?"

Jennifer and I left Cedric behind with his sister and retraced our steps to the streetcar. Pearl and George had disappeared, probably in search of a ghostly speakeasy, which was fine with me.

"Too bad Cedric isn't alive to show us around," Jennifer said.

"The only reason we met him, or rather I met him," I corrected myself, since she couldn't see him, "is because he's dead."

"Oh, right."

"At least we were able to call the police so they could start the investigation. And I'm glad Nadine didn't have to find her brother's body when she was alone. But I say we put that all behind us right now." I glanced at my phone and grinned. "We can still make it to our jazz brunch at Commander's Palace." Thank goodness I'd dressed appropriately.

One more streetcar ride and a short walk took us to Commander's Palace, a New Orleans landmark in the middle of the tree-lined Garden District. We stepped inside the restaurant and were transported to a world of timeless elegance.

A jazz trio played "As Time Goes By," as we were led to our table and handed menus. I ordered a Sazerac, considered the official cocktail of New Orleans, and Jennifer opted for a Peach Basil Cooler. When I ordered turtle soup as my starter, Jennifer wrinkled her nose.

"There's no turtle in their turtle soup," I said. Despite her obvious relief, she ordered gumbo, which she pronounced delicious.

"As good as Chef Emile's?" I asked.

"Of course not. Although, I've never had him cook for me."

"No, but he supervised my cooking very carefully. 'No shortcuts!' he used to bark at me." I sighed at the memory. "It's times like this that I really miss him. I'd love to go back home and be able to tell him all about our trip."

Three hours later, as we left the restaurant happy and full, I suggested we take the streetcar back to our hotel for a nap. "Otherwise, there's no way I'll be able to stay up past ten p.m., and I want to enjoy some of the nightlife while we're here."

MY PHONE, BUZZING ON THE NIGHTSTAND, AWAKENED me from a weird dream where Pearl, George, Cedric, and I danced the Charleston in a huge dance hall. That part was fun. It was the dancing alligators and the bouncing boudin balls that made it so strange.

The phone had stopped buzzing, but then it started again. A quick glance showed a Louisiana number, so I answered.

Nadine's voice came through the speaker. "The police aren't doing a danged thing to find out who killed my brother."

"Oh." Maybe I shouldn't have answered the phone until I was fully awake. "They've quit trying to say it was a heart attack?"

"I called that detective back, and he says it looks like the head wound didn't come from hitting his head on the table after all. That means he really died on account of somebody hitting him on the back of the head."

My mind went to the statue that I'd seen on the floor near Cedric's body. "I'm sorry, Nadine. You must be in shock."

"I knew it wasn't a heart attack. I just knew it in my bones."

"Well, now that it's been ruled a homicide, I'm sure the police will investigate." I did my best to sound reassuring.

"There've been a bunch of break-ins in the area, he told me. He figures Cedric caught them in the act and got beaned."

"That certainly sounds like a possibility." Since Cedric didn't remember what happened to him after his friend Jimmy Joe left, that didn't seem out of the question. "But you don't believe it?"

"How'd the burglar know where to find Cedric's stash?"

"Nadine." I sighed. "The cash was under the mattress. If I were a burglar, that would be the first place I'd look."

She huffed into the phone. "What about the talisman you said they took? Why would a stranger steal it?"

"A stranger might have thought it was worth something. I'm not sure it was even worth what he paid for it."

After a long silence, Nadine's voice came through softer than before. "I don't know why I called you. I thought you might be able to help."

"How? I don't—"

"I bet Sally killed him. She knew I was coming to visit today and figured her golden goose was about to be cooked."

That was interesting information. "How long were you gone?"

"I moved to Atlanta about five years ago. Me and Cedric kept in touch, but I haven't been back to town since last summer. I bet she was milking him for his money and figured I'd get in her way."

"But why kill him then?" I'd have to find out if there was an insurance policy and who was the beneficiary. "If you have any evidence, you should turn it over to the police."

"It's just a feeling I have, a strong feeling."

"In your bones?"

"If you went to talk to her, I bet you could find out what really happened. Talk to her long enough and I'll bet you'll find the crack in her story."

"Nadine, Sally's hardly going to talk to me after you told her I was Cedric's new girlfriend." I sighed, wondering what it was that made people ask me to solve murders. "I'd love to help any way I can, but I can't interfere with a police investigation."

I waited for Nadine's response, but she'd hung up.

Putting the phone down, I went to splash some cold water on my face. Coming out of the bathroom, I jumped at the sight of Cedric sitting in a chair in the corner.

"How long have you been there?"

"Long enough to hear you're not gonna find out who killed me."

Feeling the need for backup, I called out for Pearl, but she didn't appear. Instead, there was a soft knocking on my door. I opened it to find Jennifer looking as fresh as a spring breeze in a colorful dress and sandals, her hair in a high ponytail.

"Come on in." I caught my disheveled reflection in the closet mirrors. "I woke up to a call from Nadine, who's upset I'm not helping solve Cedric's murder, followed by Cedric who's also upset with me for not helping solve his murder." I pointed to the chair where he sat. "He's right there."

Jennifer sat on the edge of the bed and spoke to him. "I'm sure the police will do a thorough investigation."

Cedric scowled at her, then at me.

For some reason, I felt the need to defend myself. "Nadine says they think it was a burglar who'd been targeting the area, which is totally plausible."

Jennifer turned to me and frowned. "That doesn't sound like what I would call a thorough investigation."

"They've had a number of break-ins in the area. I'm sure they'll check fingerprints to make sure it's the same person who hit Cedric over the head."

Jennifer didn't like my explanation. "But in the meantime…?"

Cedric sprung out of his chair and began pacing. "Yeah. In the meantime, somebody could be getting rid of the evidence."

"What evidence? The only thing we know that was stolen was the talisman. And we don't even know that for sure."

"Somebody could be getting rid of it while we sit here doing nothing."

"We," I gestured to Jennifer and me, "are not doing nothing. We are going to enjoy our short vacation in your beautiful city."

My frustration grew as I found myself once again in the position of explaining to a ghost that I wasn't qualified to solve a homicide. I plopped on the sofa next to Jennifer, who listened to me tell Cedric I had no training or experience.

"You kinda do," she said. "I mean, you have helped solve a few murders."

"A lot of help you are," I grumbled. "Do you really want to spend our few days here going from dive bar to dive bar asking people we've never met about the murder of someone you don't know and can't even see?"

"Hey," Cedric said. "I'm sitting right here."

Jennifer grinned. "It might be fun."

As if on cue, Pearl came into view. "What might be fun?"

"Pearl's here," I told Jennifer. "You used her summoning word, apparently. Although, I don't think solving a murder is her idea of fun. I picture her dancing the Charleston and swigging bathtub gin."

"That's where you'd be wrong, sister." Pearl sashayed over to where Cedric sat and perched on the arm of his chair. "Don't you worry 'bout a thing. If April May can't figure out who done you in, I will."

Cedric raised his eyebrows. "Oh, you will, will you?"

She gave a coy one-shouldered shrug. "I might have already solved the case."

"You've solved the case?" I jumped to my feet. "Why didn't you say so? Who's the killer?"

Pearl smiled like a cat that had just swallowed a canary. "That little vixen, Sally."

CHAPTER 10

edric jumped to his feet, knocking Pearl off the arm of his chair. He glared at her where she sat on the floor. "Sally is the sweetest gal I ever met. She can't kill a spider, and you're saying she killed me? And besides…"

"Besides what?" Pearl picked herself up, smoothed her dress, and fussed with her hair in the mirror. "Besides the fact that you took out a big fat insurance policy?"

Cedric stared at the floor. "Wasn't that much. A hundred thousand doesn't get you much in this economy."

Pearl let out a whoop. "A hundred g's? What I could do with that kinda money. I'd buy me a full-length mink coat—one that went right down to my ankles. Or maybe a roadster. Or maybe—"

"Cedric is right, Pearl," I said. "Things have changed a lot since the last time you went shopping for a mink coat. The house would be worth at least two or three times that, maybe more. I'm not familiar with the local real estate market."

"Is that so?" Pearl returned her attention to Cedric. "Who's getting the house, Cedric?"

He squirmed in his chair. "There are extenuating circumstances, and I was just getting around—"

"Getting around to telling us?" Pearl planted a hand on one hip. "What kind of extenoo... extenoo.. What kind of circumstances?"

"Sally's getting the house?" I guessed.

Jennifer watched and listened, trying to keep up. "That's going to look pretty suspicious if he changed his will right before he was murdered. The police are going to want to know why."

Cedric fell back into his chair and gazed up at me with sad eyes. "She's having my baby."

My jaw dropped open, and it took me a moment to speak. "Sally's pregnant?" I wasn't sure why that was a shock. Plenty of women Sally's age had successful pregnancies—she just didn't seem the maternal type.

"Horsefeathers." Pearl tapped one foot impatiently. "That dame ain't no more 'with child' than I am."

"Do you have evidence that Sally isn't pregnant?" I asked. "Or is it just your woman's intuition?"

"Sure, I got plenty of—"

"Look." Cedric interrupted. "Sally isn't going to get the house. I never got around to changing my will. I guess I thought I'd live to a ripe old age like my pa. He lived to be ninety-seven."

Even if Sally wasn't getting the house, that still left the life insurance policy. A hundred thousand dollars would be enough motive for some people, though I wasn't going to tell Cedric that. At least not until I had proof.

"He didn't change his will," I told Jennifer before turning back to Cedric. "Does that mean Nadine gets the house?" I asked Cedric. "Or someone else?"

"Nadine's my only kin."

"I have a question." Jennifer spoke to the chair, which I knew appeared empty to her. "Does Sally know that the will wasn't changed?"

Cedric answered her sounding offended. "What are you suggesting?"

I knew exactly what she was suggesting. "You wouldn't be the first person to tell someone you were going to do something and not follow through." My fiancé had made a lot of promises he didn't keep, and I knew he wasn't unique in that way.

Cedric got up from his chair and headed for the door. "I'm not hanging around listening to you talk bad about my girl." He stood in front of the door and stared at it. "Can you open the door, please?"

"You can go through it," I said. "You're a ghost, remember?"

He stared at the floor and mumbled, "I don't know how."

"How'd you end up in my room a little while ago then? I didn't let you in."

He considered my question for several seconds. "I just thought about being here and talking to you, and here I was."

"So, think about being on the other side of the door," I suggested.

He stared at the door some more before I got tired of waiting for him to leave and opened it.

Pearl called after him. "See ya later." She turned back to me. "Now that he's gone, we can get back to the fun."

"Fun? Oh, right." Had Jennifer really said she thought it would be fun to investigate a murder when we could be touring New Orleans? "But Pearl, we only have a few short days to see the sights, go shopping, and eat delicious food."

"You can eat delicious food *and* find out who murdered Cedric. I bet he knows the best places to eat."

Cedric must not have gone far, because I heard him call through the door. "I know the best of the best. Not those touristy, overpriced places, either. I'll take you to a joint with the best barbecue in all of Louisiana. If there's a heaven, they gotta serve Mama Maisie's ribs."

The idea of barbecued spareribs made my mouth water, but it wasn't time for dinner yet after our three-course brunch.

It was time for a snack, and I told Jennifer so. "Let's go to Café Du Monde. I could use a café au lait for a pick me up. And maybe a beignet or two."

I took my clothes into the bathroom to change and make myself presentable. With the humidity, there wasn't much I could do with my hair, so I pulled it into a loose bun.

When I emerged, Pearl greeted me with, "Don't you look nice," probably trying to get on my good side for some reason. She always seemed to have an ulterior motive, which made me reluctant to trust her.

I grabbed my purse and yanked the door open. I let out a yelp when I nearly ran into Cedric, who stood waiting for us. Jennifer and the two ghosts followed me down the hall.

"Where's George?" I asked Pearl.

She huffed. "With some trollop at Arnaud's plying her with bathtub gin. I told him I never wanted to see him again and came right back here." She nudged Cedric. "Where'd she say we're going?"

"Café du Monde."

"What are we going to find there? Clues? Evidence?"

"Cafe au lait."

"Café...? But that's just coffee." Pearl sighed. "Although, I wouldn't mind a cup o' joe. Not having a body, partaking in food and drink is more like tasting a memory."

As we waited for the elevator, I told her, "You don't have to tag along."

"Huh?" Jennifer gave a confused look.

"Not you," I said. "Pearl."

"Are you dismissing me?" Pearl puffed her red lips into a pout. "Listen, Miss High and Mighty. Just because you're all alive and everything doesn't mean you can solve Cedric's murder without us."

"Of course we need Cedric, but what help do you think you're going to be?" I asked. "Besides distracting me?"

"Sugar, I can go where you can't. I can see things you can't."

Cedric nodded. "She's got a point."

Pearl seemed to think that settled the matter.

JENNIFER AND I STEPPED ONTO THE STREET, NEARLY blinded by the bright sun.

Pearl nudged Cedric in the ribs with her elbow. "Let's ditch these two stiffs and see what we can find out on our own."

Cedric looked from her to me and back to her before saying, "You can go. I'm sticking around a bit longer."

"Okay by me." Pearl took his arm, and they strolled off in the same direction we were going. Loud music came from the wide-open doors of bars and tourists crowded the sidewalk, many of them holding plastic cups with colorful drinks, most likely too-sweet-for-me hurricanes and daiquiris.

We'd nearly arrived at Café du Monde when I

had the sense that someone was following us. I stopped and stepped to the side to get out of the way of passersby.

"Did you forget something?" Jennifer asked.

Instead of answering, I pointed at Detective Bowman's partner coming our way. He looked out of place in the French Quarter in his suit and tie.

"Oh, hello." He tried his best to be nonchalant, but I wasn't buying it.

Pearl's eyes widened. "I remember him. What's he doin' here?"

"You're Bowman's partner." I tried to remember his name. "Officer…"

"*Detective* Azemar." He gave me a pleasant smile, but his voice was stern. "And you're April May, if I recall correctly. It's an easy name to remember. And your assistant…"

I turned to Jennifer. "Why don't you grab us a table and order me a café au lait?" She hesitated, so I did my best to reassure her. "I'll just be a moment."

She narrowed her eyes at Azemar before agreeing and leaving us to talk.

I folded my arms over my chest and did my best to look as stern as he sounded. "Why are you following me?"

"What makes you think I'm following you?" he asked. "Or a better question might be, why might I, a homicide detective, want to follow you, the person who just happened to arrive in town just in time to find their new friend's dead body."

What was he implying? "If you have something to say, why don't you just say it."

"What were you really doing at Cedric's home this morning?"

I resented the implication that I had something to do with Cedric's death. "I already explained why I was there. We met online, and he was nice enough to offer to show us around town."

"Here's the thing," he said. "I went through Mr. LeBlanc's emails, texts, and other correspondence and saw no mention of your name. Your number wasn't in his phone."

How was I going to explain that? I glanced over at Cedric, but he was no help. Pearl only shrugged. "Maybe he used a different phone."

"So, if I looked at your phone, I'd see calls to a New Orleans area code?" He held out his hand. "Mind if I check?"

"Yes, I do mind. I know my rights." At least I hoped he would need a warrant to search my phone. But would he need one to check phone records?

"Mm hmm... Either you tell me what your real involvement was with the deceased, or I will bring you in for questioning. I can hold you for forty-eight hours without charging you."

"Is that so?" I didn't like being threatened, and that was how I felt. "What would Detective Bowman have to say about that?" I had a strong feeling Azemar wasn't talking to me on Bowman's instructions. He might not even know what his junior partner was doing. "I wouldn't have a lot of hope for your future prospects after my lawyer gets in touch with your chief of police."

Cedric grinned. "That's the way to talk to a bully. Not that I would ever talk to a police officer that way, but hey."

The detective stood tight-lipped and silent, not meeting my eyes as I waited to find out what he'd say next. I didn't have to wait long. "They've arrested an ex-con for the rash of burglaries that have occurred in the area. We've been able to connect him to several of the burglaries, and he has no alibi for the night of Mr. LeBlanc's death, so it looks like the D.A. is going to charge him in that case."

I began to understand why Detective Azemar was harassing me. "You don't think the burglar killed Cedric, do you?"

"Not for a second."

"I don't either." I could hardly tell him I got my information from the ghostly realm. "And I'm glad someone's keeping the investigation open."

"That's just it. It's not going to stay open for long unless some new information comes to light."

"That's where I come in?" I guessed.

"You're right about my partner." He huffed out a breath. "My *senior* partner. I can't investigate openly —not without risking his wrath. We're working at least twenty cases right now, and he would lose it if he found out I was working on a case that he'd thinks he's already solved." His bravado seemed to have disappeared as he allowed me to see his frustration.

I felt for him, but I wasn't about to let my guard down. "You don't really think I had something to do with his death, do you?"

He pursed his lips. "I hoped you had some information that I could use to convince Detective Bowman to keep the case open."

Cedric waved his arms. "Ask him about the talisman."

"If Cedric surprised a burglar, then why wasn't anything valuable stolen?" I asked the detective. "I don't think that talisman he wore was worth much."

"We don't know for sure what was stolen. According to his fiancée, there was quite a bit of cash under the mattress, but she couldn't give us an exact amount."

"His fiancée? You mean Sally?" I scoffed. "That's the first person I'd suspect of killing Cedric. You must know about the insurance policy."

He raised his eyebrows, and I wondered if I'd said too much.

"Sally has an alibi," he said. "She was with someone all night."

I glanced at Cedric before asking the detective, "When you say she was with someone you mean…?"

"Yes," he said. "She was with a man. All night."

CHAPTER 11

*D*eputy Azemar gave me his number and asked me to call him if I had any information I thought might be useful. "Or anything you haven't shared with me yet."

I didn't want to lie to him, or anyone else for that matter, but I wasn't about to tell him I had been hanging out with Cedric's ghost all day.

As we walked away, Pearl tried to console Cedric. "I'm sure Sally had a good reason for being with somebody all night."

"Not just somebody," Cedric said morosely. "A man."

Pearl gave me a long-suffering roll of her eyes as she patted Cedric on the arm. "Honey, for all you know, she coulda been with her brother. Or an uncle."

He perked up slightly. "You really think so?"

"Sugar, anything is possible." She took his arm. "I know a little speakeasy right around the corner.

How about we have a little nip and talk things over."

"Good," I muttered as they headed down the street. "It's about time I had a little peace and quiet."

Jennifer had snagged a table for two on the edge of the Café du Monde patio where a mug of chicory coffee and steamed milk waited for me. A nearby saxophone player serenaded tourists with bluesy jazz tunes.

While we waited for our beignets, I quietly updated Jennifer on my conversation with Azemar.

"He knows something is fishy about my story, but I'm pretty sure he'll never guess that I've been hanging out with Cedric's ghost."

"What do you think he'd say if you told him?"

"I can only guess, but I don't for a moment think he'd believe me. And lying to a police detective about a murder case could get me into hot water. Or he might think I'd lost my mind."

Our beignets arrived, and Jennifer grabbed one, making happy sounds with each bite. I didn't blame her. They were light, airy, and delicious.

She swallowed and pointed at me. "You've got some powdered sugar on your chin."

I laughed. "You do too. And your cheeks. And your shirt."

She shrugged and took another bite, mumbling, "Oh, who cares."

"I'm not sure I can eat all this. If we come back, we'll share an order."

She shook her head playfully. "I don't want to have to fight you for the third beignet."

The chicory coffee had revived me, not to mention the sugar. "Did you know they started adding chicory to coffee during the civil war when there was a coffee shortage?"

"I didn't. But I like the way it tastes. It's really strong but not too bitter."

Minutes later, I stared at my plate, not sure what had happened to the beignets I didn't think I could finish. I sipped my coffee and pondered how we could help find out who had killed Cedric, assuming a burglar hadn't killed him like Bowman thought.

"Do you think the talisman is an important clue?" I asked Jennifer. "Cedric's friends would have known it wasn't worth enough to kill for, so unless we come up with a different motive, we'll have to eliminate them as suspects."

"Eliminate who?" Cedric appeared out of nowhere. For someone who couldn't figure out how to walk through doors or walls, he was pretty good at materializing out of thin air.

"Your friends."

"Are you telling me you think Jimmy Joe had something to do with my death? Or Maurice? You're out of your mind."

I spoke to Cedric while staring at my coffee in case someone, especially Azemar, was watching us. "Jimmy Joe's the last person who saw you alive, right?"

"He's my best friend in all the world. He'd do anything for me. And vice versa."

"And who's the other guy?"

"Maurice sold me the talisman. Said it was worth a whole lot more than $200, but he knew I could use the luck. He was right, too, 'cuz that's when everything started lookin' up for me."

Until you died.

Almost as if he could hear my thoughts, his face fell. "Didn't protect me in the end, though."

Jennifer stood up and brushed the powdered sugar from her lap. "Sounds like we need to go talk to Jimmy Joe."

A donkey-driven carriage clomped by as I watched it longingly. Jennifer and I could be riding one just like it with a guide telling us all about the history of the French Quarter.

Instead…

Pearl came toward us, with George hurrying to catch up. "Hey, Cedric. Why'd you take off?"

George called after her. "That woman means nothin' to me. I was just having a little fun is all. Can't a bloke have a little fun?"

Cedric said to Pearl, "We're gonna go talk to my buddies. Jimmy Joe was with me that night. He mighta seen something."

"Fine," I said, tired of arguing with him. "We might as well get it over with." I stood and threw away my trash before turning to Cedric. "It's around four-thirty. Where do we find Jimmy Joe?"

"That's easy." Cedric grinned. "He'll be at Pete's."

"The bar?" I guessed. "No surprise there, I suppose."

I told Jennifer where we'd find Cedric's buddies, and she agreed we should go talk to them. "They might not even know he's…" She paused.

"It's okay," I said. "Cedric knows he's dead."

She grimaced. "I don't want to be disrespectful."

As we walked the few blocks to Canal Street, sweat dripped down my back. I remembered the phrase, "It's not the heat, it's the humidity."

Uptown was the last area I would have chosen for us to spend our vacation. After all, we had all the French Quarter to explore, not to mention Jackson Square, City Park, and several museums. We could be on a river boat or a swamp tour right then, and I said as much to Jennifer.

As the streetcar chugged through the Central Business District, Jennifer did her best to help me see the positive in the situation. "It's an adventure, April. How many people get to have a ghost show them around town while they hunt down clues and question suspects?"

"But it's your first trip out of California, and you've hardly seen anything other than the inside of a streetcar."

Jennifer wasn't listening. Along St. Charles Avenue, commercial buildings and hotels had given way to the Garden District. I followed her gaze out the window at the elegant and stately homes that had been built in the nineteenth century.

"They're so beautiful," she whispered, a million miles away. "Imagine what it must have been like to live back then. The clothes, the traditions, the balls..." She tore her eyes away from the window, turned to me, and sighed. "Although I do like having flush toilets and antibiotics."

"And big-screen TVs. And pocket-sized computers that we carry around with us."

Jennifer raised her eyebrows, and I held up my phone. "When I was growing up, a room-sized computer couldn't do half of what this can."

Pearl, who'd been standing next to the driver for the best view strode back to us. "I bet they threw some swell parties back in the day."

"Still do," Cedric said. "Not this time of year, though. People who own these houses have enough sense to wait until after hurricane season before they come back to town."

Was that a dig at me for choosing to visit in September? "The weather has been quite pleasant on our visit." I wiped my brow. "Besides, I prefer to visit when it's less crowded."

Pete's Pit Stop wasn't far from Cedric's home, and the whole trip gave me a strong sense of déjà vu. The bar shared the first floor of the two-story structure with a convenience store.

"Ready?" I asked Jennifer. When she nodded, I pushed on the wooden door and we stepped inside, waiting a moment as our eyes adjusted to the lack of light. It was the sort of neighborhood bar you might have found anywhere in the country, except for the umbrellas hanging upside down from the ceiling and the Zydeco music playing over the loudspeaker.

The place was almost empty, not surprising considering the time of day. The bartender, a wiry man with a shaved head and several visible tattoos, moved behind the bar with the efficiency of someone who'd been doing it for a decade or two. He didn't acknowledge our presence, perhaps thinking we'd wandered in by mistake and would leave as quickly as we'd appeared. One man sat at either end of the bar, almost as if they'd been sent to opposite corners after a fight.

Cedric called out gleefully to a middle-aged man with thinning hair and a weathered face at the far end of the bar. His baggy t-shirt and cargo shorts hung on his frame. "Hey, Jimmy Joe. *Laissez le bon temps rouler.*" He tried to slap his friend on the back, but his hand went right through him. This must have reminded Cedric of his ghost status, because his mood darkened.

Jimmy Joe shivered, a reaction I often noticed when people unknowingly encountered ghosts. I knew first hand it wasn't a pleasant feeling.

I pulled out two stools and took a seat, leaving an open spot between Jimmy Joe and me. Jennifer sat on the other side, looking very much out of place. A chalkboard listed the daily specials.

"Is it still Tuesday?" My nap had disoriented me.

Jennifer confirmed the day. "And according to the board, it's Tequila Tuesday."

Cedric leaned over my shoulder. "Nine-dollar pitchers of Abita. That's beer, if you didn't know."

The bartender, possibly disappointed to see we hadn't left yet, ambled over. "Margaritas are two for twenty."

"That sounds—"

"Don't." Cedric said, stopping me before I ordered. "No margaritas. Bill uses the cheapest tequila this side of the border. Not sure it's really tequila, come to think about it. It'll give you a headache the likes of which you never seen."

"That sounds good," I told the bartender, "but I think I'll have a gin and tonic."

Jennifer ordered a Coke. While Bill got our drinks, I pointed out Jimmy Joe to Jennifer while doing my best not to be obvious. He stared into his beer, but was his expression mournful? Guilty? Bored?

Jennifer leaned close and whispered. "How are you going to go about questioning him?"

"I'll play it by ear, unless you have a better suggestion."

By the time we got our drinks and paid for them, I had decided the direct approach would be the best, or at least the quickest. "Are you Jimmy Joe?"

His head jerked up and he gave me an open-mouthed stare. In a slow, lazy drawl, like a man who has all day to say what he wants, he asked, "Who wants to know?"

"You heard, I suppose." I watched his expression, but it didn't change. "About Cedric?" Did he know he was the last person to see his friend alive? Before the murderer, that was.

"Heard what?"

Cedric gave me an accusing glare. "Don't play him like that."

I glanced at the bartender, who'd stopped pretending to wipe glasses, then turned back to Jimmy Joe. I hadn't expected to be the one to tell him his best friend was dead. Why didn't I think this through before I opened my big mouth?

"I'm so sorry." I genuinely meant it. "Cedric died sometime during the night."

CHAPTER 12

Jimmy Joe stood up so quickly his stool fell to the floor with a loud clunk. "What are you talkin' about. Ah just saw Cedric yesterday."

I sighed and glanced over at Jennifer who only shrugged. Meanwhile, Cedric looked angry enough to spit.

"I found him this morning at his house. The policeman who came said he thought it was a heart attack." I fished in my purse for the card Officer Bowman had given me and handed it to Jimmy Joe. "I'm sure he can give you more information." I didn't want to be the one to tell him his friend had been murdered.

He snatched the card from my hand and pulled out his phone. As he dialed, he walked down a hall that I guessed led to the back door or the restrooms, or maybe both.

"Nice goin', April," Cedric said to me before hurrying after Jimmy Joe.

Jennifer and I had become much more interesting to Bill. "That true? Cedric is really dead?"

"I'm sorry to say, yes."

"JJ's going to take it hard."

"JJ?"

"Cedric started calling Jimmy Joe that and it stuck. Them two was like two peas in a pod, always singing from the same hymn sheet."

"What was Cedric like?" Jennifer asked. When the bartender gave her a suspicious look, she added, "I never got to meet him."

Bill gave the question some thought before answering. "A good guy. Loyal. Shared what he had when he had it, which wasn't that often, but still. Tipped good. Too trusting sometimes." He lowered his voice. "Especially when it came to Jimmy Joe and Maurice."

"Maurice?" I asked, pretending I hadn't heard the name before.

The bartender narrowed his eyes. "You didn't know Cedric too well, if you never heard of Maurice."

"We connected online. We didn't get the chance to meet in person, actually." In a hushed tone, I added, "I never got to see him alive." I had begun to regret that fact.

"You okay, JJ?" Bill asked when Jimmy Joe reappeared from the back of the bar, pale-faced and visibly shaken.

He picked his stool up from the floor and sat, taking a long drink of his beer. "Cops said somebody killed him. Probably a burglar."

Cedric turned to me, his voice urgent. "Maybe Jimmy Joe saw someone coming when he left my place last night. Maybe he saw whoever murdered me."

That was my thought too, but how was I going to bring up the subject? I figured I'd at least give it a try in a roundabout way.

"When was the last time you saw Cedric?" I asked.

Bill must have thought it was a question for anyone to answer. "He was here last night. Wish I'd known it'd be the last time I ever saw him. He had a couple beers and a bacon cheeseburger and then went home to watch the end of the game, 'cuz he said it got too loud in here. Around seven, I think. And you left a little bit after that, right, JJ?"

"Huh?" Jimmy Joe had the look of a deer in the headlights. "Yeah. Ah went straight home."

Bill huffed. "I never said you didn't."

Cedric's brows drew together. "What you talking about, JJ? You came by to see me. Don't you remember?"

Jimmy Joe couldn't hear his friend, of course. Should I confront him about his lie? Maybe in private would be better.

"This must be such a shock for you," I said, doing my best to sound soothing and non-confrontational. "I'm wondering if you know anything about his talisman."

"How'd you know about that?"

"He told me he wore it all the time. Said it brought him all kinds of luck. It's gone missing."

"That goober." Jimmy Joe scowled at his beer. "Maurice got it in one of them tourist shops for ten bucks and sold it to Cedric for two hundred. Two hundred!" he repeated as if he couldn't believe anyone could be that naive. "No burglar would think that thing was worth anything."

Cedric stared at his friend in disbelief.

I said what I figured Cedric was thinking at that moment. "I thought Maurice was his friend."

"Yeah, he just thought it was funny. Can't trust a guy like Maurice. See, there are different kinds of friends. Maurice is the kind of friend you have a few beers with, not the kind you trust with your money or your girlfriend."

"Did Cedric trust his girlfriend with Maurice?" I asked.

Jimmy Joe's face reddened. "Nah, Sally was off limits. Everyone knew that."

The bar began to fill up with regulars who all seemed to know each other. One by one, they learned about Cedric's death, which required buying a round of drinks and many toasts to their late departed drinking buddy.

I wanted to stay until Maurice showed up, but after an hour, I figured we'd need to order another drink or food if we were going to stick around.

"Maybe he's not going to show up tonight," I said to Jennifer, assuming she'd know I meant Maurice. "Why don't we go somewhere and get dinner?"

She smiled with relief. "I was hoping we weren't eating here."

Jimmy Joe was surrounded by his buddies, so I figured he wouldn't care much if we left without saying goodbye. I pulled out a card, planning to give it to the bartender, but before I did, the front door flung open. Half the people in the bar called out, "Maurice!"

Maurice, who stood at least six-feet tall, held his arms out in greeting. "Heya!" His gray-blond hair was rock-star shaggy, and his tanned, prematurely aged skin gave him a rugged look. He wore a tan vest over a white, long-sleeved shirt open at the neck and the cuffs rolled up.

Jennifer gave me a wide-eyed look. "That's Maurice?"

"Guess so."

She shook her head as if in awe. "He's got to be at least forty, but..." She sighed. "He's..." She didn't finish the sentence, but I knew just what she meant.

"He sure is," I agreed. Something about him was effortless, and I had a feeling he knew exactly the effect he had on others, especially the ladies.

One of the regulars rushed over to him talking and waving his arms around excitedly. Maurice appeared confused at first and looked around at the others for confirmation. His gaze stopped at Jimmy Joe, and he raised his eyebrows in a question.

Whatever non-verbal signal had passed between them, Maurice's face fell, and he made his way to his buddy.

"Tell me it's not true," Maurice pleaded.

Jimmy Joe said nothing. Nothing needed to be said.

CHAPTER 13

This page intentionally left blank.

(I'm not superstitious, but why take chances?)

Jennifer and I agreed to stay put a little longer to see if we could talk with Maurice. As he and Jimmy Joe talked, he must have learned than I was the one who brought the news about their friend's death.

As he headed towards us, I could tell his attention was on Jennifer.

"Ladies." His face flickered between grief and a practiced smile. "My name is Maurice Landry. I am…" He paused. "That is, I was a good friend of Cedric. My buddy JJ says you had the unfortunate occasion to discover his body."

"I'm afraid so," I said. "I'm very sorry about your friend. I'd only started to get to know him."

He raised one eyebrow. "Is that so?"

"We connected online over our love of baking. I own a tea shop in California. Oh, I'm sorry I didn't introduce myself. I'm April and this is Jennifer, my—"

"Charmed, I'm sure," he said, taking Jennifer's hand in his. I half expected him to kiss it. "How long are you visiting the Crescent City?"

Jennifer glanced over at me as if not sure what to do. "Um, we're flying back on Friday."

"No, that can't be. I've just met you and now you're going to leave? You'll be back, though, no doubt."

Jennifer smiled tight-lipped and shrugged, seemingly unable to speak.

"Perhaps you could be persuaded to go to dinner with me. I'm sure your mother—"

"Boss," I corrected.

He grinned. "Oh, I see." He focused his attention on me. "What do you say, boss? Can you spare Jennifer for an hour or two before you whisk her away back to California?"

"I don't think—" I began.

Jennifer interrupted. "I'd like that."

Maurice grinned, all signs of grief erased. "Wonderful. What is a good time tomorrow?"

I stepped in. "We've already made plans to go to the art museum tomorrow."

Maurice gave in a little too easily, I thought. He took a card from his vest pocket and presented it to her with a flourish. "If you change your mind, lovely lady, give me a call. I'm afraid I need to…" He gestured to Jimmy Joe, who wiped his eyes with a paper napkin.

I waited until we got outside to ask Jennifer what she was thinking. It was still light outside, thank goodness. I didn't want to be walking at night in an area I wasn't familiar with.

"Just think of what I might learn if it was just the two of us." Jennifer insisted she'd be safe going to dinner with Maurice, but I was far from convinced. "I am an adult, you know."

"And Maurice is a murder suspect. I don't like the idea of you going out with him at all, but I can't tell you what to do." I glanced back at the door of Pete's Pit Stop. "I guess Cedric is staying behind with his friends. I hope he doesn't get stuck on the mortal plane. It seems like the longer ghosts take to move on, the harder it becomes. Or maybe less appealing." My stomach growled, and I pondered our choices for dinner. "We could find someplace to eat nearby if you're super hungry."

Jennifer eyed the low hanging sun. "I'd like to get back to the French Quarter before it gets dark, if that's okay with you."

"I agree." At least she was being sensible about that.

After some discussion as we rode the streetcar back, opted to try Napoleon House, which we'd passed by earlier that day. When we arrived, we were led to a table by the window looking onto Chartres Street.

We both ordered versions of a Pimm's Punch, which I'd previously thought was only popular in England. While we waited for our drinks, I asked Jennifer what she thought about Jimmy Joe and

Maurice. "Did their surprise and grief seem genuine to you?"

"Jimmy Joe sure seemed surprised. But why did he say he hadn't seen Cedric after he left the bar last night?"

"Good question. I'd like to talk to Jimmy Joe when he doesn't have an audience. I'm guessing Cedric will know where to find him during the day."

The server set our drinks down and took our order. I suggested the charcuterie board, but Jennifer made a face when she saw it included alligator sausage. Instead, we chose to start with Italian cheesy bread, followed by two orders of red beans and rice.

By the time our food arrived, Jennifer stared at the dishes. "I don't know if I can eat all this after our huge brunch."

"We'll just have to do our best."

We needn't have worried. Whether it was all the walking we'd done or the tasty food, we ate nearly every morsel.

After dinner, we strolled along Chartres Street. The sidewalks were crowded, considering it was hurricane season. It might not have been the best time to come, but so far, we hadn't gotten much rain. More importantly, there were no hurricanes forecasted during our stay, though that could change quickly from what I'd been told.

I spotted Arnaud's French 75 bar. "How about a cocktail? I've heard the bar is nice."

"Can I get a Coke?" Jennifer asked.

I chuckled. "You can get whatever you want."

We entered and found a Queen Anne style sofa and chairs empty in one corner as if waiting for us. Cedric sat next to me on the sofa, which made it easier to talk to him without attracting attention.

"Are there any pictures of the talisman?" I asked him. "Maybe we can find out more about it."

"Doubt it." He made a sour face. "I'm not one of those millennials taking selfies of myself." He glanced at Jennifer. "No offense intended."

"You know she can't hear you."

He chuckled. "Yeah, I forget sometimes, though."

"What?" Jennifer gave me a worried look. "What did he say?"

"Just a disparaging remark about millennials. Nothing you haven't heard plenty of times, I'm sure."

"Doesn't bother me at all. I'm Gen Z."

CHAPTER 15

We walked back to the hotel in silence as my mind worked busily on a plan, or at least the semblance of one.

Jennifer nudged me. "You have an idea, don't you."

"You can draw." Jennifer had so many talents, sometimes I wished I had a little of her artistic abilities.

"And you can bake." Jennifer grinned. "When we get home, you're going to have to make beignets, you know. Especially when I tell Irma about them."

I chuckled. "You're probably right. But what I was thinking is that if Cedric could describe the talisman, then you could draw it."

"Oh, right." She gave me a sheepish grin. "I thought it was an odd comment, but sometimes…"

"Sometimes?" I laughed. "Anyway, do you think you could?"

She shrugged. "I can try. But I don't have any art supplies."

"Maybe not." I grinned. "But we can fix that in the morning, say nine o'clock?" I'd already scoped out all the places I thought Jennifer would like to visit, including an art supply store, smack dab in the middle of the French Quarter.

NOLA Arts Supply Shop would be our first stop the next morning after breakfast.

THERE WERE NO GHOSTLY VISITORS TO MY ROOM THE next morning, and I managed to sleep until nearly nine. It wasn't until we'd finished our breakfast of bacon, eggs, and creamy delicious grits and were heading for NOLA Art Supply when Cedric appeared.

He walked alongside me. "Any progress finding out who killed me?"

"Well, at least we now know Sally has an alibi, so that means we can focus on other suspects."

He scowled. "That's not progress. I told you she had nothing to do with my death. Any lead on somebody who might have actually killed me?"

It didn't seem polite to tell him my top two suspects were his best friends, so I sidestepped the question. "I wish I'd been able to talk to Jimmy Joe alone. You heard him say the last time he saw you was at the bar. And we both know that's not true."

"Oh, sure, but you gotta understand. JJ's got

some history with the police. The last thing he wants is to be on their radar. You know how it is."

I had history with the police of a different sort. "Not exactly, but you know him better than I do. I just think he might have seen something when he was leaving. Do you know where we can find him? Maybe if Bill the bartender isn't hovering nearby, he'll tell us the truth."

"You might be right about that, but he works on Tuesdays until four. Or is it Wednesday? Anyway, he works Wednesday, too. But then he has three days off."

I checked my phone to double check the day. "Today's Wednesday." I didn't want to wait another day, especially since we were leaving on Friday. "Can we maybe stop by and talk to him on his break?"

He shook his head. "Nah, it's not that kinda place. You wanna get him fired or something?"

I ignored his question. "And Maurice? Where does he work?"

Cedric's brow knit together at the name. "Who knows where he goes during daylight hours?" He added with a grumble, "I can't believe he scammed me."

Was Cedric being purposely unhelpful? I doubted it. More likely, he wasn't ready to believe that one of his friends might have had a hand in his death.

I relayed the information to Jennifer who had a question of her own. "Do you think someone will know something about the talisman that will help? I have a feeling it's important, even though it wasn't worth much."

"It's definitely worth checking out," I said.

As we turned the corner, we came upon George and Pearl.

"There you are, doll." Pearl took Cedric's arm. "Why the glum face? We're in *New Orleens*. This town was made for fun—not for moping."

"They're back," I said to Jennifer, then addressed Pearl. "Cedric has lived here his whole life. I think he knows what the city has to offer."

"Does he now?" she said with a flirty smile. "For your information, Miss Flat Tire, he's new to our side of the veil, and there are juice joints he never saw when he was alive."

George grabbed Cedric's arm. "C'mon, fella. We'll show you around."

Pearl took his other arm and the three of them headed down the street. As they turned a corner, I had a pang of worry for Cedric.

I shared my thoughts with Jennifer. "Do you think he's okay with those two?"

"He's already dead," she said. "What else could happen to him?"

That was a question I couldn't answer.

We soon arrived at the art store, where Jennifer meandered down every aisle of the cramped shop. Meanwhile, I perused the greeting card selection and did my best to be patient. When she appeared with her arms full of supplies, she told me in no uncertain terms that she was paying for them.

"But—" I began to object, but she held up a hand to stop me from saying more.

"It's enough that you're paying for the entire trip." She must have thought she sounded too harsh, because she softened her voice and added, "Which I appreciate very, very much."

After she paid, I asked if she needed to stop by the hotel to drop some things off.

She claimed the huge bag of art supplies wasn't heavy. "I wanted to draw the talisman, but I guess we'll have to wait until Cedric comes back. Is there somewhere special you wanted to go?"

"Can we go back to Café du Monde?" The beignets were calling me, especially after she said I needed to learn to bake them when we got home. It was just a few blocks away.

As we arrived, I gestured toward the far end of the cafe. "I don't know how he knew where to find us, but he's here."

We ordered our café au laits and beignets to go and found a place to sit away from potential eaves-droppers. Cedric joined us, eyeing our food longingly as Jennifer pulled out her sketch pad and pencils.

Cedric described the talisman, and I repeated his words as Jennifer began to sketch.

"It's about two inches. Round. Gold toned."

Jennifer measured and drew a nearly perfect circle.

"Oval-shaped red stone in the middle," he said, and I repeated. "Funny little marks, like squiggles."

"Like the letter S? Or like snakes?" she asked.

"Sort of like an S, but a snaky S."

We went back and forth, with Jennifer fine tuning the sketch until Cedric approved. She put the final touches on the sketch and handed it to me.

"Was there anything on the back?" I asked.

"That's the odd thing." Cedric's brows drew together. "The back was mesh, and it looked like it would slide open, but I never could figure out how."

"Do you think something might have been inside in a secret compartment?"

"Like what?" he asked. "It wouldn't have held much."

"It could be almost anything as long as it was small enough to fit. A note or a picture perhaps?" If there was something hidden in the talisman, was that what got Cedric killed?

CHAPTER 16

$\mathcal{W}$ith the drawing completed to Cedric's satisfaction, Jennifer stared at it as if it might reveal a clue. Her ever-present smile began to fade.

She looked at me hopefully. "How this sketch going to help us find Cedric's murderer?"

"Good question," Cedric said.

I wish I felt more confident that it would, but it was all we had. "According to Jimmy Joe, Maurice got it from a tourist shop. Maybe we can start there."

Jennifer brightened. "I saw a bunch of them right around here. We can show them the drawing and see if anyone recognizes it."

Cedric began pacing back and forth, waving his arms around as he spoke. "I don't see how going from one tourist trap to the next is gonna help find who killed me. We don't even know which shop he got it from or even if Jimmy Joe knew what he was talking about."

"What else do you suggest?" I didn't care for his attitude, considering we were giving up our vacation time to help him. "I'd like to question Jimmy Joe, but according to you, we can't talk to him until after four. And you don't know where Maurice is. I wouldn't mind talking to Sally, but I'm pretty sure she doesn't want to talk to me after your sister told her I was your new girlfriend."

"Nadine didn't mean nothin'. She's just protective, that's all."

"Since you think asking around about the talisman is a waste of time, we might as well head over to the art museum so Jennifer can see her fashion exhibit. We can walk around City Park while we're there." I turned to her. "Did you know it's bigger than Central Park in New York?"

"Actually, I did know that. And I've heard they have oak trees that are almost eight hundred years old."

"Wow. I can't wait."

As we cleared off our table and threw away our trash, Jennifer watched me to find out how Cedric was reacting.

"There's a botanical garden, too," I commented. "I wouldn't mind seeing that if we have time."

As I led the way to the streetcar that would take us to City Park, Cedric offered a sort of apology.

"It's just hard for me, you know?" he whined. "I

can't do nothin' on my own, and you're the only one who can see me."

"You're lucky you got me. Think what would have happened if I hadn't happened to be in town. You wouldn't have had anyone to talk to other than ghosts, and there's not much help they can give you."

"Yeah." He hung his head. "You're right. I guess asking around about the talisman is about the best plan we got at the moment."

The best plan? It was the only plan.

CHAPTER 17

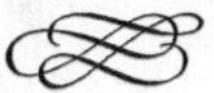

The dark clouds gathering ominously overhead told me it could start pouring any minute.

"Maybe you should go ahead to the museum. I'll stop in a few places and see what I can find out about the talisman and meet you there later."

She narrowed her eyes. "Are you sure this isn't just a scheme to get out of going? If you don't want to go, you can just say so."

I laughed. "Yes, I ordered those black clouds. There's an app for everything these days."

"That's not what I meant," she said, a slight whine in her voice. "Besides, I don't know how to get there."

"I'll walk you to Canal Street. You'll take number 48 to the end of the line, and from there, it's a short walk to the museum." I handed her one of the passes I'd bought.

Once Jennifer was on her way, Cedric guided me

through the streets of the French Quarter like a man on a mission. Our first stop was the Vampyre Boutique where he said a "mystical priestess" named Madame Morgana had "great spiritual power."

Was this the same shop where Freddie had bought the talisman I'd been wearing since she gave it to me? So many shops had similar names, I couldn't be sure.

I had my doubts about a so-called priestess who would operate out of such an obvious tourist trap, but we had to start somewhere.

We stepped inside the tiny storefront. The shop, filled with tee-shirts, voodoo dolls, candles, and other souvenirs, had room for about eight people max.

A man wearing a top hat and dreadlocks sat behind a glass case overflowing with rings, necklaces, and silver daggers. I asked if Madame Morgana was in.

"Nope."

I pulled Jennifer's sketch out of my bag. "Have you ever seen a talisman like this?"

He stared at it for a long moment before answering, "Nope."

It seemed unlikely that I'd get any information out of him if I kept asking yes or no questions.

"What time do you expect Madame Morgana will be in?"

"Can't say."

Glancing over at Cedric, I jerked my head to suggest we leave.

"That was a bust," he said as he followed me out to the street. "Too bad, cuz she's the real deal. She might even have been able to tell you who killed me."

That sounded doubtful, but I kept quiet. "We can come back later and see if she's in." I guessed that she worked the evening shift when there were way more tourists out and about, especially drunk tourists willing to part with cash in exchange for having their fortune told.

As we walked along Dauphine Street, we passed a jewelry shop. I doubled back, thinking it wouldn't hurt to stop in.

"Good thinking," Cedric said. "That talisman mighta been worth more than Jimmy Joe thought. Maybe Maurice didn't scam me after all."

Next to the door was a button. I pressed it, and a friendly voice said, "C'mon in," accompanied by the sound of a buzzer.

I pushed the door open and stepped inside the small shop. An elegant, older woman with a steel-gray bob greeted me from behind a glass counter filled with gold jewelry.

Not wanting to waste her time, I set the sketch of the talisman on the counter and gave her my warmest smile. "If you have just a moment, I wonder if you wouldn't mind taking a look at this sketch. It's a pendant that's gone missing, and I'm trying to track it down. I figured it might help if I knew if it was valuable or not. I'm guessing not, but I'd like to be sure."

She returned my smile and picked up the drawing. "Interesting. What do you know about it?"

"Not much," I admitted. "My friend said it was a voodoo talisman of some sort, maybe something they sell in the tourist shops."

"Doubtful." She held the sketch at arms' length then set it back on the counter. "It appears to be a Victorian-style pendant, something that might have been popular in the late eighteen hundreds. Typically, the metal would be eighteen or twenty-two karat gold and the gemstone..." She glanced at the sketch again and pursed her lips. "It could be a ruby, but more likely it was a garnet. Garnets were quite popular at the time."

"Victorian?" I glanced at Cedric, who shrugged. "Does that mean it might be valuable?"

"That's hard to say without seeing it. Reproductions don't usually have that level of detail, so if it's a genuine and in good condition, it could be worth anywhere from a few hundred to several thousand. Much more if that gemstone is a ruby."

"Wow."

"If your friend had no idea of its worth, I'd wager it's on the low end of that scale, but you never know. I've had locals bring in jewelry that was worth a great deal more than they expected, usually after the death of an elderly relative. Did he inherit it?"

"He got it from a friend." If it was worth thousands, I couldn't believe Maurice would sell it to him for two hundred.

The woman interrupted my thoughts. "Is there anything else I can help you with?"

I shook my head. "Thanks so much for your time."

"If you retrieve it, I'd love for you to stop by and let me see the real thing. I'd be happy to give your friend an idea of its value and perhaps make an offer if they're willing to sell."

"I'll keep that in mind."

We stepped outside and I looked up the location of the nearest pawn shop.

Cedric hovered nearby looking smug. "I knew Maurice didn't get it for ten bucks."

"Let's not jump to conclusions. For all we know, it might be an inexpensive reproduction." Real or not, I wondered how Maurice procured it. "You never did say what Maurice does for a living."

"What?" He seemed preoccupied by the possible value of his trinket. "Oh, he does whatever to get by. He's not a nine-to-five kinda guy, if you know what I mean."

"I have an idea." I paused, hoping my next question didn't upset Cedric. "Is he a buy-stolen-property kind of guy?"

He took it in stride. "Nah, nothing illegal." He tapped his chin as he seemed to reconsider. "Although..." He didn't bother finishing his thought.

I pointed down the street. "Next stop, Dixie's Pawn Shop."

Cedric brightened. "Cool. I know the owner."

"Dixie?"

He chuckled. "Nah, his name is Doug. He thought Dixie's Pawn Shop sounded better, so that's what he called it."

I passed by antique shops, boutiques, and a cozy-looking bookstore, wishing I could stop in to browse. What had happened to my vacation? The next time I went out of town, I would make sure that George and Pearl didn't follow along. They were trouble magnets.

The pawn shop on the edge of the French Quarter had an air of disrepute despite being situated next door to an art gallery.

The door creaked as I pushed it open and entered the dimly lit shop. Flickering amber lights cast long shadows. The walls and shelves were cluttered with all manner of items, from mirrors, artwork, and musical instruments to machinery and tools.

Behind a glass case overfilled with jewelry and watches stood a thin man with slicked back salt-and-pepper hair. As I approached, his lips curled into a half-smile, revealing a gold tooth that gleamed under the dim lights.

"Looking for something in particular?" he asked with a hint of a drawl.

Cedric came up next to me. "That's not Doug."

"I hoped you could tell me if someone brought it

in a pendant. My friend is very upset that he lost it, so I'm helping him track it down. It has a lot of sentimental value."

His smile faded, but he took the sketch I held out. After a quick look, he said, "Haven't seen anything like that come in lately."

"No?" I wasn't sure he was taking me seriously. "Can you take a closer look?"

"I don't have to. Not much jewelry being pawned lately other than wedding rings. Mostly big screen TVs, guns, and electric guitars. But you might ask Doug."

Right, Doug, the owner. "Is he in?"

He gave his head a quick shake. "Always off on Wednesdays."

"Will he be in tomorrow?" What was it with people in this town? It seemed as if I had to pry every tidbit of information out of them piece by piece.

"Yeah. He'll be here all day."

I thanked the man and left. As I stepped out into the bright sunlight, Cedric slipped through the door before it shut.

"I guess there's nothing more to do until we can talk to Jimmy Joe and Maurice again."

"Are you sure? Maybe you can give one of those detectives a call."

"No way." I wanted to stay off their radar as much as possible. "I'm going to meet up with Jennifer at the art museum."

As I headed for the streetcar stop, Cedric stayed

behind, unhappy with me for going off to enjoy my vacation. As soon as I found my seat on the Canal Street streetcar, I sent a text to Jennifer, letting her know I was on my way. She didn't answer, which made me think she must have muted her phone so she didn't disturb others at the exhibit.

I imagined her slowly making her way through the museum taking in all the historical details on every item of clothing. It wasn't that I didn't like learning about history, but I loved the stories more than the dry facts. Like the stories Chef Emile used to tell me about where he grew up in Louisiana.

The streetcar traveled through dramatically different scenery. Gone were the stately homes of the Garden District, the colorful cottages and shops of the French Quarter, and the high rises of the business district. Instead, I saw a mishmash of office buildings, banks, and other businesses interspersed between Victorian homes, bungalows, and apartment buildings.

As I stepped off the streetcar in front of City Park, the warm, damp air hit me, thick with the scent of freshly cut grass. The tracks rattled behind me as the streetcar pulled away and I crossed the street and entered the park. The trees overhead stretched their long branches across the sky, casting dappled shadows on the walkway.

Another text to Jennifer went unanswered. I reached the museum, climbed the stone steps, and entered the imposing structure. For the next half hour, I went through the exhibit, then through all the other rooms, only glancing at the paintings and sculptures.

I began to worry. Had something happened to Jennifer on the way to the museum? Had she left for some reason?

Returning to the museum lobby, I entered the café to wait for her to contact me. I heard her laugh—at least it sounded like her.

The moment I spotted her sitting with her back to me, my relief was replaced by annoyance when I saw who else sat at her table.

Maurice.

CHAPTER 18

Two glasses of wine sat half-empty on the table.

I glared at Maurice and tried to control my tone of voice as I said to Jennifer, "I've been trying to text you for at least the past hour."

Maurice must have seen the anger flashing in my eyes, because he became very apologetic. "Please forgive me. It's all my fault."

"You bet it is. Who do you think you are—"

Jennifer said in a loud whisper, "April, people are staring. I ran into Maurice and asked him to join me for a glass of wine. It's not his fault."

"But it is," Maurice insisted. "I came here today hoping to run into you."

I pulled out a chair and sat down. "Sorry. I got really worried and when I saw you I kind of…"

Jennifer finished my sentence. "Went ballistic?"

"That's perfectly understandable," Maurice said, once again pouring on the charm.

I didn't trust him.

I SHIFTED UNCOMFORTABLY IN MY SEAT ON THE streetcar as it rattled down Canal Street. The late afternoon sun filtered through the window, casting long shadows. Across the aisle, Maurice sat with his legs casually stretched out, taking up more room than necessary and leaning closer to Jennifer than I liked.

I focused on the scenery rushing past them— anything to avoid having to engage with Maurice. There was something about him I didn't like, though I couldn't quite place it. Maybe it was the way he'd conveniently showed up at the museum, or perhaps it was how comfortable he seemed with Jennifer, as if he had known her for far longer than he had.

Looking through my phone at the notes I'd made for the trip, I got busy making plans for the evening that wouldn't include Maurice.

"You okay, April?" Jennifer asked, snapping me back to reality. "You've been quiet."

I offered a tight smile. "I was just thinking. It's been a long day."

"Well, hopefully the night'll be more fun," Maurice said. "The Quarter comes alive about this time of day."

"I'm sure it does, but we'll be hanging around dead people."

Jennifer's eyes widened while Maurice appeared only mildly intrigued.

"We have tickets for this evening for the St. Louis Cemetery Tour."

WE STEPPED THROUGH THE CEMETERY GATES CLOSE ON the heels of our guide. I tugged my sweater closer, trying to shake the creeping chill that seemed to rise from below ground.

Jennifer spoke in a whisper. "This is supposed to be the most haunted cemetery in New Orleans. What were you thinking?"

"I'm not sure I was thinking," I whispered back. "I was trying to come up with a polite way to ditch Maurice. I'm sorry, I know you like him, but—"

"Like him?" she asked, louder than she probably meant.

Several people in front of us turned to glare at her and one older woman said, "Shush."

"Sorry," Jennifer said, back to whispering. "He's charming, sure, but he's also manipulative, shallow, inconsiderate…"

I missed the rest of her adjectives as our tour guide, a tall, sturdy woman with a raspy voice and a heavy Southern drawl waved us forward. "Alright, y'all. Stay close. St. Louis Cemetery is famous for its history, but it's also known for the restless spirits who never quite made it to the other side. Now, let's not wander off. You never know who—or what—you might run into here."

Jennifer leaned in closer to me as we followed the group through the winding paths between the above-ground tombs. The atmosphere felt heavy, the air thick with an odd, faint scent of flowers mixed with decay. The stone crypts stretched upward, some chipped and weathered by time, others freshly restored. It felt like a maze of the dead.

My mind wandered, only half-listening to the guide's tales of infamous figures buried there— voodoo queen Marie Laveau, eccentric millionaires, and forgotten victims of disease. But the familiar tingle at the back of my neck pulled my attention elsewhere.

"Oh no," I muttered under my breath, sensing the faintest flicker of energy around us.

Jennifer glanced at me, concerned. "What is it?"

Before I could respond, the chill sharpened, and a familiar, cackling laugh echoed through the silent cemetery. I closed my eyes and sighed.

"Not here, not now," I whispered, but, of course, they never listened.

"Dollface, you didn't think you could come to the cemetery without inviting us, did you?" The voice was unmistakable—George, with his gleeful mischief.

"Darlin', we wouldn't miss this for the world," Pearl's chainsaw voice cut in, as she materialized next to George. Pearl's red dress shimmered under the ghostly moonlight, and George, with his pinstripe suit and cocky grin, looked every bit the roguish gangster he had been in life.

"George and Pearl?" Jennifer asked under her breath. When I nodded, she bit back a laugh. "Of course they're here."

I grimaced, glancing around to make sure no one else could see the ghosts. But of course, the other tourists remained oblivious, listening intently to the guide's story about a phantom who supposedly roamed the cemetery at night.

Jennifer gave me a nudge. "Relax, it's just George and Pearl. What could they really do?"

"Do you want a list?" I kept my eyes trained on George as he drifted toward the guide.

Pearl, meanwhile, floated gracefully beside us, her expression suddenly more thoughtful. "Y'know, these tombs… they remind me of old times. I can still picture the parties we used to throw. George used to know all the best spots in town, didn't you, sweetheart?"

"Yep," George called back, poking his head through one of the tomb doors. "But we never hung around too long. No point getting attached."

April felt a pang of sympathy as she watched Pearl. For all their playful banter, there was a sense of longing in her voice. The dead were still bound to the living world in ways they could never fully explain, and Pearl's wistful gaze at the tombs made that clearer than ever.

Suddenly, the guide stopped, her face pale. "I…

I think we should move along quickly, folks. It's getting… chilly out here."

The others oohed, and some giggled, going along with what they thought was all for show, but I knew differently. George, his arms wrapped around the tour guide, winked at me, clearly pleased with himself.

As the group shuffled toward the exit, I shot a stern look at George and Pearl. "That's enough for tonight. We're leaving."

Pearl gave an exaggerated sigh. "Spoilsport. Fine, fine. But next time, we're leading the tour."

George tipped his hat and smirked. "Pleasure as always, doll."

THE NEXT MORNING, JENNIFER KNOCKED ON MY DOOR shortly before eight. She seemed somewhat less enthusiastic than usual as she plopped herself on a chair.

"It's pouring rain." She heaved a dramatic sigh, and I had to stop myself from laughing.

"It rains a lot in the south. Remember what you said? At least it's a warm rain."

"Yes, but just like dry heat is still hot, warm rain is still wet. And you can't wear a raincoat because it's too warm, but if you actually remember your umbrella, there's a good possibility you'll leave it somewhere and have to buy another."

"So, you're saying we should move to New

Orleans and open an umbrella shop?" I hoped to coax a smile from her, but she only sighed again. "We can still go to some of the museums you wanted to see."

"You're just going because I want to."

"Yes, that's what friends do on vacation. In life, too, come to think of it. It's all give and take. We got to go to Commander's Palace like I wanted, and now we'll visit some museums, like you want."

A man's voice called my name from the other side of the door.

"Cedric is here," I said to Jennifer as I went to the door to let him in. As he entered, I told him, "You know you can walk through doors, right? You're not solid."

"Easy for you to say." He plopped down on the bed. "So, we going to back to Dixie's?"

"Dixie's?" It took me a moment to remember what he was talking about. "Oh, right. The pawn shop."

"The owner's gonna know something, I have a real good feeling about it. The other guy said he'd be in today, right?"

I didn't want to waste any more of our vacation chasing after dead end leads. "It's our last full day to see all the sights, and Jennifer has more museums she wants to visit. We're flying home tomorrow, remember?"

Jennifer nudged my arm. "I can be on my own for a little while if you want to stop by Dixie's with Cedric."

"Are you sure?"

"It'll give me a chance to visit The Cabildo, which I know would bore you to death. Did you know it was once the seat of the Spanish Government?"

"Spanish? I thought New Orleans was French until the Louisiana Purchase." I was proud of myself for remembering anything from high school history class.

"Spain ruled Louisiana for nearly four decades. They gave it back to the French just a few months before France sold it to the U.S. The building is historically significant, and I've heard the exhibits are a must see for history buffs."

"I'm surprised you didn't become a history teacher." My assistant never ceased to amaze me with all her knowledge.

"I'm considering it, but I have at least two more years of school before it's time to decide what to do with the rest of my life. How do people manage to pick just one career when there are so many possibilities?"

"Sometimes the right choice appears before you like magic."

AFTER GRABBING MUFFINS TO GO FROM THE HOTEL dining room, Jennifer and I parted ways. It was a short walk to Dixie's Pawnshop, but long enough for Cedric to nag me about what else I planned to do to solve his murder.

"One step at a time, okay?" Although if this lead didn't pan out, I didn't have a clue what to do next, other than to join Jennifer at whatever museum she'd discovered.

Doug, the owner of Dixie's Pawnshop, gave me a quick nod, his gruff demeanor matching the worn, no-nonsense look of his shop, as if he'd seen it all and wasn't impressed. His sharp eyes took in every detail of the sketch.

"Yeah, a guy brought in the talisman but when I told him what it was worth, he left."

"Was it a guy named Jimmy Joe?" I asked.

His eyes narrowed. "I wouldn't stay in business long if I gave out my customers' names anytime a stranger came in asking."

"Of course," I said with a friendly smile. "But I'm not exactly a stranger. I'm a friend of Cedric's. He's the one who sent me in to see you."

"I see." He scratched his chin. "I thought the guy looked familiar."

"You'd seen him with Cedric before?"

A hint of a smile told me I was right.

As we stepped outside, I turned to Cedric. "We need to talk to Jimmy Joe, and I'd rather get it over with now. You said he's not working today, right?"

He nodded. "I can take you to his house."

After texting Jennifer, Cedric and I headed to the streetcar to take us back to uptown.

Uptown. Where no one spent their New Orleans vacation. No one except me.

Jimmy Joe lived in a modest shotgun house not far from Pete's Pit Stop. I banged on the door, then turned to Cedric. "Will you go in and see if he's inside? I don't want to leave until we know for sure he's not here."

"But how?" Cedric stared at the closed door, still unable to convince himself he could go right through it.

I sighed. For once, I wished George or Pearl were there to show him the ropes. "You're a ghost, Cedric. See?" As much as I hated doing it, I put my hand right through his upper body. It was an icy sensation that always gave me the willies.

"Hey." Cedric scowled at me. "Don't do that."

"Then go through the door." None of the ghosts I'd met had explained how they moved through walls, but it couldn't be that hard. "Why don't you start by pressing your nose up against the door."

He gave me a skeptical look, then stepped up to the door. "Like this?"

"Exactly, now—"

"Whoa!" Cedric disappeared through the door in a flash. He called to me from the other side. "That was a rush. I haven't had a trip like that since that one time in 1999…"

His voice faded away, and I took a quick look

around to make sure none of the neighbors were watching before calling through the door. "Now go see if Jimmy Joe is in there."

A message dinged on my phone. Jennifer wanted to know how much longer I'd be. I gave her the best answer I could: *Soon. Will update shortly.* If Jimmy Joe wasn't at home, I'd try to talk to him later in the evening at Pete's Pit Stop.

Cedric reappeared, apparently having finally mastered going through solid objects. "He's still sleeping."

"Does he usually sleep in this late?" It was nearly ten o'clock.

"Dunno. Maybe he's taking a nap. I tried to shake him, but, well... you know." He headed down the walk. "Let's come back later."

An unsettled feeling in the pit of my stomach wouldn't let me leave. Stepping off the concrete steps, I tiptoed around sad-looking rosebushes, careful to avoid their thorns until I came to a sash window. The screen came off easily, and I pushed up on the window, but it didn't budge. The window next to it didn't open either.

As I made my way around the side of the house, I hoped the neighbors were at work and not watching me trying to break into Jimmy Joe's house. Thankfully, the third window opened easily.

Looking around for something to stand on so I could climb through, I caught a whiff of a familiar odor: methane, or more accurately, mercaptan, the compound added to natural gas to give it a distinctive odor so that a leak could be detected by smell.

I pulled out my phone and called for help. When the police arrived, I'd have to do some fast talking to keep them from putting me in cuffs and hauling me away to jail.

I'd tell them that Jimmy Joe had called me… no, they could check his phone. Maybe we'd agreed to meet, or he'd invited me over to help with the funeral arrangements? No, Nadine would be handling that, or maybe Sally.

Moments later, a white police SUV pulled to the curb and two uniformed police officers got out, one female and one male. The woman headed straight for me while the other stayed back.

"We got a report of a break-in." She looked around, obviously not considering that I might be the possible burglar.

Before I could respond, a woman emerged from the house next door with a baby on her hip pointing an accusing finger at me. "That's her. She tried to break into Jimmy Joe's house. Arrest her."

I held back a sigh. "Jimmy Joe asked me to come by today, and when he didn't answer the door, I thought I smelled a whiff of gas. I wasn't sure, so I started trying to open windows. When I got this one open," I pointed at the side window that stood partially open, "I got a lungful."

She followed me to the window. It only took one sniff to confirm my story. As she went back to her car, the neighbor hovered nearby, probably hoping for some juicy gossip to share with her neighbors.

The equipment that had been retrieved turned out to be gas masks and carbon monoxide detectors. One of the officers climbed through the window and opened the front door.

As I stood by the open front door, one officer opened windows while the other beelined for the back of the house.

I heard her call from the kitchen. "The pilot light was left on."

The other called from another room. "We've got a body."

A few curse words might have escaped my lips. Why did I have to be the one to always find the bodies?

CHAPTER 19

Cedric's mouth hung open. "I thought he was sleeping." A tear slithered down his cheek. "Jimmy Joe. Why'd you do it?"

Leaning in through the doorway, I didn't see Jimmy Joe's ghost, but that didn't surprise me much. After all, I couldn't see most ghosts, thankfully.

My heart sank when Bowman and Azemar arrived, although I shouldn't have been surprised to see them. I half expected them to arrest me on the spot. Instead, Bowman asked me about Jimmy Joe's frame of mind lately while his partner looked on.

"You think he killed himself?" I asked. "No way. I mean, I didn't know him that well, but he just didn't seem the type." That sounded unconvincing even to me. "And besides, why would you decide to end it all, turn the gas stove on, and then go lie down at the other end of the house? To give yourself plenty of time to change your mind? That doesn't sound right."

Bowman grunted. "We'll know more once we get the tox screen results, but we found an empty bottle of sleeping pills on the nightstand."

I stood near the door to Jimmy Joe's bedroom and looked in. If I didn't know better, I'd have thought he was peacefully sleeping.

Cedric stood next to the bed, leaning over him, his face wet with ghostly tears. "Why can't I see him?"

Not able to speak out loud, I gestured to the body. Was he having problems with his vision?

"Not his body. Him. Where'd he go?"

I shrugged. Maybe Jimmy Joe had hurried off to explore the afterlife. The few ghosts I'd met hadn't come back to tell me who or what had greeted them when they finally accepted they needed to move on.

"Is there any relevant information you have to share before you leave, Ms. May?" Bowman asked.

I hesitated. I wasn't ready to go, but I was obviously being dismissed. "Jimmy Joe knew more than he was saying about who killed Cedric."

Bowman raised his bushy eyebrows. "Do you have any evidence to support that theory?"

"Yeah. I'm pretty sure he tried to pawn Cedric's talisman—the one that went missing the night he died."

"That might explain why he killed himself," Bowman said. "Couldn't handle the guilt."

"The guilt over stealing a worthless piece of jewelry?" I asked.

"The guilt over murdering his friend." Bowman's condescending voice made it sound like that was the obvious conclusion.

I wasn't so sure. "Maybe. He might have thought the talisman was worth something. The guy at Dixie's Pawn Shop told him it wasn't worth much after all. That must have been a huge disappointment. Did you find it here?"

"Not yet, but we'll do a thorough search just to make sure."

"Would you let Nadine know if you find the talisman? She might want it back." Though why she'd want a worthless trinket was beyond me, especially if she thought it had brought her brother bad luck.

I stood on the sidewalk and composed a text to Jennifer before deleting it. A phone call would be more appropriate.

She answered with, "Where are you?"

"I'm in front of Jimmy Joe's house." Before she could say anything else, I blurted out, "He's dead."

"Dead? Please tell me it was natural causes." She sighed loudly. "Never mind. I know better."

"I'm sorry I've left you on your own so long."

"I would make a joke about the extent you'll go to avoid going to museums, but it's too sad. I kinda liked Jimmy Joe. He was a character."

"He was."

"I'm leaving The Cabildo, and I just realized I

haven't had anything to eat except a muffin, and that was hours ago. Have you eaten?"

My stomach growled at the thought of lunch. "Want to meet somewhere in the French Quarter? Cedric says Mama Maisie's has the best barbecue this side of the Mississippi."

"I don't think they use that phrase in New Orleans, since the river goes right through the city."

"Okay, Ms. Geography Expert," I teased. "Did you have something else in mind?"

"Could we get red beans and rice again?"

"Sure." Checking my phone, I reviewed the list of restaurants I'd researched before the trip. "I'm almost positive Muriel's has red beans and rice. It's near Jackson Square. Give me an hour." I hoped that would be enough time to get back to the French Quarter.

As I ended the call, I turned at the sound of high heels coming up the sidewalk.

"What's goin' on?" Sally swung her hips side to side as she stepped carefully on the uneven pavement. She gave a worried look at the ambulance and police car. "Is Jimmy Joe okay?"

I shook my head. "I'm sorry, Sally. Jimmy Joe is… he's gone."

"What do you mean, gone?" Her eyes widened as she began to understand. "You mean he's dead? Jimmy Joe can't be dead."

Thinking about her condition, I kept my voice calm. "This must come as a shock to you. Do you need to sit down?"

"No, I don't need to sit down." She scowled at me as if I were an annoying gnat. "I need to find out what happened. Who can I talk to?"

"A shock isn't good for the baby," I blurted out before I thought better.

"Baby?" She narrowed her eyes. "What baby?"

"Aren't you having Cedric's baby?" My voice wasn't much more than a squeak.

"No, I'm not having Cedric's baby."

"Jimmy Joe's?"

Her face turned bright red, and I backed away slowly, a little afraid she might hurt me. She turned and stomped to Jimmy Joe's house and up the stairs.

I took the opportunity to hurry down the street, leaving Cedric to witness whatever Sally was about to dish out to the detectives.

It began to drizzle, and I scolded myself for leaving my umbrella at the hotel. For some people, rain activated their curls, but for me, it meant frizz. I pulled a scarf out of my pocket and tied it over my head, feeling very old fashioned, and not in a good way.

As I walked along Napoleon Street, a prickle ran up the back of my neck. I stopped, pretending to look at my phone. Glancing over my shoulder, I felt some relief to see a familiar face.

"Following me again, Detective Azemar?"

"Who said I was following you?" he asked, not appearing the least bit guilty to be caught. "It's a lovely afternoon for a stroll."

Gazing up at the darkening sky, I held out my hand as huge raindrops began to fall. "You call this a lovely afternoon?"

"You're from California, right? I hear it never rains there."

"It never rains. But it does pour." He, of course was far too young to remember the song, but my mother often sang it every time it rained.

"Do you have time for a coffee?" he asked. "There's a little place around the corner that's one of my favorites."

I considered asking him what this was about, but he seemed relaxed and non-confrontational, so I decided not to be difficult. Also, a coffee and a dry spot in a cafe didn't sound terrible.

The coffee shop, housed in a blue and white New Orleans-style cottage, looked promising from the outside. The interior couldn't have been cozier, especially on a rainy day, with throw rugs and a brick fireplace in the corner.

I ordered a rose cardamom latte, and we took our drinks to a pair of leather chairs. Before taking a sip of my drink, I took a picture as a reminder to ask Jennifer to recreate it.

Impatient to find out what Azemar wanted, I asked, "Why did you want to talk with me, Detective?"

He took another sip of his drink before answering. "I feel like we started off on the wrong foot. Please don't take this the wrong way, but I can't help but think you know more than you're telling us. It seems to me, you've been very careful not to lie, exactly, but you've left out some details."

"I've told you everything that's pertinent to either case. Or rather, Cedric's murder, since you and Bowman don't think Jimmy Joe's murder was the result of foul play."

"Bowman doesn't. I'm not so sure."

"Oh good." I felt my shoulders drop a bit, surprised at how grateful I felt to hear him say that. "This morning, I was convinced that Jimmy Joe must have killed Cedric since he had the talisman, but then who killed Jimmy Joe? By the way, did you find it?"

"The talisman? We didn't find anything like what you described."

"I think if you find that talisman, you'll find the killer."

"Is that so." Azemar's expression was unreadable. Did he have his own theory about who murdered Cedric and Jimmy Joe?

Azemar kept talking as Cedric walked through the closed door of the coffee shop and headed our way, looking pleased with himself. "It's kind of fun to walk through doors and walls once you get the hang of it." He looked from me to Azemar and back before crumpling his forehead. "What's going on here?"

I tried to ignore him and focus on what Detective Azemar was saying.

"...you seem to know a lot about Cedric, who you claim you never met, and Jimmy Joe, who you met only briefly. And you seem unusually interested in Cedric's murder. Are you one of those true crime junkies who interfere with law enforcement? Because the way things are going, Bowman is going to throw you in jail if he even thinks you're getting in his way."

"Thanks for the warning." I tried but failed to keep the sarcasm out of my voice.

"A warning you should take seriously."

Azemar seemed open-minded, at least more than Bowman, but what would he say if I told him why I knew so much about Cedric and his murder?

I leaned back in my chair. "I care about Cedric. If I thought you and Bowman were on track to solve his murder, I would be happy to step back and let you do your jobs."

His brows drew together, and his voice became defensive. "I'm doing everything I can to solve this case."

I leaned forward in my chair and lowered my voice. "Then why are you here with me? You should be talking to Maurice."

"Maurice? Why?"

"That's who sold Cedric the talisman in the first place. Jimmy Joe said it wasn't worth what he paid for it." I stopped, my mind telling me something didn't add up. "Doug at the pawn shop said it wasn't worth much either. It's almost like everyone is trying to convince us that it's worthless. Which makes me think..."

"That it's far from worthless?" Azemar nodded

his head thoughtfully. "What's the name of this pawnshop?"

"Dixie's. Doug is the owner." I stood. "Thank you for the latte, Detective. I'm off to meet Jennifer for lunch at Muriel's."

He had a faraway look. "I love their red beans and rice."

I sent a text to Jennifer to let her know I was running late and hopped on the streetcar. The walk to Muriel's took another fifteen minutes, and by the time I arrived, she'd already gotten a table.

"I ordered their burrata appetizer," she said as I took a seat across from her. "I hope that's okay."

"It's always okay to order burrata." The creamy cheese made from mozzarella and cream was a favorite of mine.

I ordered their signature Fleur De Lis cocktail and began filling Jennifer in on what had happened in the short time since I last saw her.

"Do you think Detective Azemar suspects something?" she asked.

"Like that I can see Cedric's ghost? More likely he thinks I'm covering up for someone or even that I'm involved somehow."

"He couldn't possibly think that." Jennifer paused as if trying to read my expression. "Could he?"

"He could."

After a wonderful meal, I had an idea what to do with the rest of the afternoon. "Shall we walk off our meal and maybe do some shopping?"

Jennifer grinned. "I thought you'd never ask."

As we walked back toward the heart of the French Quarter, Cedric appeared. His head hung low, weighed down by the burden of his grief.

"I can't believe Jimmy Joe is dead," he said. "Two murders. And you're no closer to finding the killer."

"It's not my job, Cedric."

Jennifer must have sensed the ghost and I needed to resolve a few things. "Why don't I check out this shop and let you two talk." She ducked inside a boutique.

A low voice startled me. "What does she mean, you two?" Azemar stood with his arms crossed wearing a suspicious expression.

How does he always find me? "Did you put a tracker on me?"

He scoffed. "You have a very vivid imagination."

That wasn't exactly a denial, but I let it go. "How'd it go at Dixie's? Did you learn anything?"

"A thing or two. Do you remember what the owner told you?"

I thought back and tried to remember Doug's exact words. "He said that a guy wanted to sell him the talisman, but when he told him what it was worth, he left. He wouldn't tell me the guy's name, but I was pretty sure it was Jimmy Joe."

"Your detective skills need a little work, Ms. May." His mouth turned up slightly as if he was holding back a smile.

"What did I miss?" Repeating the words in my head, it dawned on me. "He told Jimmy Joe what it was worth, and Jimmy Joe left. Are you saying it was valuable? And that's why he didn't pawn it?"

He nodded. "Exactly. It was solid 15k gold. And Doug wasn't sure, but he thought the gemstone might have been a ruby."

"Whoa."

"Holy cow," Cedric slapped his leg. "Well, don't that beat all. And here you thought Maurice was trying to scam me."

I repeated what the lady at the jewelry store had told me. "If it is a ruby, it could be worth thousands."

Jennifer emerged from the shop. "Oh, hello, Detective." She turned to me. "Everything okay?"

"Detective Azemar picked up on something I missed. I guess that's why he gets the big bucks."

He snorted. "Yeah, right. By the way, I'd rather not share the details of the investigation with any more people than necessary." He gave Jennifer a condescending smile. "I hope you don't mind."

"Sure," she said cheerfully. "I just wanted to let April know I was going to try on some dresses. Besides," she said with the sweetest smile, "April will tell me everything later. Ta-ta!"

She gave him a little wave and slipped back into the shop while I observed Azemar's annoyance. It seemed like his previous friendly demeanor had evaporated.

"I'd like to get back to a previous subject that wasn't explained to my satisfaction," he said.

"Yes?" I had a pretty good idea what that subject was.

"How did you really meet Cedric LeBlanc? And why do you know so much about him and his friends? And let's not forget the talisman."'

I met his stare. Those beady amber-brown eyes didn't intimidate me. Much.

"You wouldn't believe me."

"Try me."

"Okay." I might as well try the truth and see how it went over. Taking a deep breath and letting it out slowly bought me a few moments before making my confession. "I can see Cedric's ghost."

CHAPTER 20

$\mathcal{I}$ waited for the laugh or snort of derision, but it didn't come.

Instead, he simply asked, "Can you prove it?"

"Prove it?" That was the last thing I'd expected him to say. "Like how? You want me to tell you his driver's license number?"

"How about his birthday?"

"Okay." Cedric gave me the date, and I repeated it to the detective.

Azemar frowned. "You could have looked that up. How about birthmarks? Scars? Tattoos?"

"I got a real good scar," Cedric said gesturing along his abdomen. "Goes from here to here. Appendix nearly burst. I coulda died, but I didn't."

"He has an appendix scar from here to here." I mimicked Cedric's gesture.

"Anything else?" Azemar asked, obviously far from convinced.

When Cedric told me about his one tattoo, it was

all I could do to keep from rolling my eyes. "It's never a good idea to get a tattoo of your girlfriend's name."

"Those could both be lucky guesses. Where is this tattoo, exactly?"

Cedric told me and I couldn't help responding, "You got her name tattooed on your butt?"

Azemar's demeanor completely changed from the tough cop to a stunned observer. "He's here right now?"

I nodded and gestured to the ghost. "Detective Azemar, meet Cedric LeBlanc."

"My mémère is not going to believe it. On second thought, she probably will." The detective leaned forward. "Tell me everything."

Where to begin? "From time to time, I can see ghosts, but only certain ones. So far, they've been murder victims, except for George and Pearl. That was a murder-suicide."

He grimaced, which surprised me. I figured he must have seen and heard everything.

"It's okay, though," I continued, "because George doesn't remember that Pearl is the one who shot him. Although, maybe if he did, he might stop fooling around with other women. Some men never learn."

"And how did Cedric enter the picture?" Azemar hurried me along, as if impatient for me to get to the good stuff.

"George and Pearl followed me to New Orleans. Pearl really wanted to fly on a plane, so…" I was interrupted by a huff. "Sorry. That's not important. Anyway, our first morning here, they showed up in my hotel room with Cedric. Although I had to open the door for him since he hadn't figured out how to walk through solid objects yet."

"And that was…. Tuesday?"

I nodded. "Tuesday morning just hours after his death. All they wanted me to do, they said, was go to his house so I could discover his body and call the authorities. But Cedric has been following me around pretty much the whole time insisting that I solve his murder." I added under my breath, "He doesn't think the police are doing a good enough job."

His frown deepened. Did he not believe me? Or was he unhappy about a ghost's opinion of his investigation?

He leaned against the side of the shop, his long legs crossed casually, as if we were two friends having a chat. "Sure wish I could talk to murder victims. It would make my job a whole lot easier."

"Not always. A lot of the time they send me in the totally wrong direction." Like Cedric insisting that no one close to him could have killed him. "They don't usually remember what happened when they died, and they're very opinionated. Cedric insists there's no way his friends or his girl-friend could have had anything to do with his death."

"Sally does have an alibi," he reminded me. "But Maurice?"

"He's a sketchy dude, and probably a fence." I smiled, remembering his handsome face. "He is charming, though."

"Uh-huh," he said, although he didn't appear to be listening.

"What are you thinking?"

"I'm thinking I'd like to take you to see my mémère? She lives just a few blocks away in The Marigny."

"The Mare-Inny?" I did my best to pronounce the name.

"Faubourg Marigny is one of the oldest neighborhoods in New Orleans. My grandmother has lived there since she and my grandfather got married. She raised her family there. What do you think?"

"About?" My head was swimming with possibilities.

He chuckled. "Stopping by to see her."

"Why?"

"Let's just say she won't blink an eye when you tell her you can see ghosts."

"Uh-huh." I had a feeling there was more to it than that. "And maybe she can tell you if I'm a fraud?"

"That did occur to me," he admitted.

"Let's go." My experiences with other people's grandmothers had always been wonderful. "I'll let Jennifer know. I'm sure she won't mind as long as she doesn't run out of dress shops."

"In the Quarter? Not a chance."

I stepped into the shop and found Jennifer, who asked for my opinion on a dress she was thinking of buying. Of course, she looked great in everything, but this was not her usual style.

"It's sort of… goth?" I said. "Not your usual sunshine and roses aesthetic."

"I thought it would be great to wear for spooky season." When I raised an eyebrow, she clarified, "You know, Halloween."

"In that case, it's perfect." I told her that Azemar was taking me to meet his grandmother.

It was her turn to raise an eyebrow. "Interesting. I can't wait for you to tell me all about it later. I'll do a little more shopping, then head back to the hotel. I could use a shower before going out again. Meet you there when you're done?"

"Sounds good," I said. "Wish me luck."

Azemar led me through the narrow streets of the Quarter as we headed east. The lively chatter of tourists and loud music faded into the background as we crossed Esplanade Avenue.

"Have you been to Frenchmen Street yet?" Azemar asked. When I shook my head, he suggested we walk that way. "If you're looking for some real New Orleans jazz music, you're more likely to find it there than in the Quarter."

I hurried to keep up with him. "How'd the street get its name?"

"It's named for the six French loyalists who were executed after leading an uprising. They weren't happy about being under Spanish rule after the Louisiana Territory transferred to Spain."

"Your town has so much history. In northern California where I live, my house is one of the oldest houses in the area and it's only a little more than a hundred years old."

"That's considered new construction around here," he joked.

We turned a corner and Azemar stopped in front of a small cottage or bungalow similar to others we'd passed along our way.

"Here we are," he announced.

I didn't know much about Louisiana architecture, but the house felt like it belonged, right down to the yellow siding and black shutters.

I pointed to the front of the house. "Why are there two doors?"

Cedric snickered. "Ain't you never seen a Creole cottage before?"

"Some people use one door for guests and one for themselves." Azemar climbed the front steps to a small porch. "On a hot day, you can open the doors and windows for a cross breeze. These old Creole cottages all had a similar floor plan, sort of like a square box divided into four rooms. Since there's two doors, a lot of them have been split into two residences."

Azemar knocked softly on the door on the right. We didn't have to wait long. The door swung open, and an elegant plump woman appeared, wearing white capris pants and a bright pink blouse. Silver-streaked curls framed her face, which broke into a wide smile.

Azemar bent down so she could wrap him in a tight hug which seemed to last a long time. When she finally released him, she gave him a playful smack on his arm.

"What took you so long to come see your old mémère?" she scolded him.

"Aw, you know it ain't been more'n a week." Azemar's accent seemed to have suddenly changed.

Cedric watched with a melancholy expression. "I sure miss my grandma."

"Mémère," Azemar said. "I brought someone to meet you." He took a step back and held out a hand in my direction. "This is April May."

"April May," she said with a smile. "I've been expecting you."

CHAPTER 21

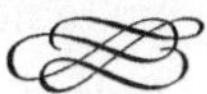

 zemar hadn't touched his phone since he asked me to come see his grandmother. When had he decided to bring me here?

"Your grandson told you I was coming to meet you?"

"He didn't tell me a thing, *chérie.*"

Under his breath, Azemar told me, "Just go with it."

"My name is Odile." She reached out her hand. "Any friend of my grandson's is welcome in my home."

"Thank you," I said as she clasped my hand in both of hers. "I'm not exactly a friend." I quickly tried to backtrack. "I'm not *not* a friend, but I mean, we aren't…"

She continued to hold my hand as her dark eyes searched my face. "Never you mind. I've got some fresh lemonade that will cool you right off."

She let go of my hand and we followed her

inside. Wood floors, polished but weathered, creaked gently underfoot. The furniture was a mix of antique chairs, old-fashioned tables, and a beautifully upholstered settee. The cottage was filled with the kind of clutter that made a house feel like a home—books stacked on tables, framed photos on the mantelpiece, and candles seemingly everywhere.

An ancient-looking hound dog slowly got up from his spot in front of the fireplace and ambled toward me.

"Don't mind Rufus," Azemar said. "That ole hound dog is older than dirt. I don't think he's got more than two teeth in his head. He might gum you to death if you're not careful, though."

I crouched down to scratch the dog's ear, but the dog seemed more interested in sniffing my shoes. Once he was satisfied, he lumbered back to his spot going around in circles three or four times before plopping on the floor. Within seconds, he began to snore.

"Your home is lovely." I took in all the details. "It almost seems untouched by time."

"Just the way I like it," Odile said, giving her grandson a pointed look. I guessed that he'd pushed her to modernize, but I was pleased she hadn't given in.

She motioned for me to sit while she and Azemar went to the kitchen. He returned shortly carrying a tray with three glasses and a glass pitcher. He set the tray on the coffee table, poured three glasses of lemonade, and handed me one.

I took a taste and closed my eyes. It tasted like sunshine in a glass, with just the right balance of sweet and tart. "Delicious."

"The lemons came right off my tree out back. They grow as big as grapefruit and they're so sweet I hardly have to use any sugar. That reminds me." She turned to Azemar. "Would you go pick some more for me?" She turned back to me. "I can't reach the high ones, and by the time they fall off on their own, they're no good."

"Sure thing, Mémère." He stood and glanced back at me, a non-verbal check-in. I nodded to let him know I'd be just fine without him.

"He's such a good boy," she said. "I figured you might feel a little more comfortable talking without my grandson the police detective hovering over us like a high-school dance chaperone. So, tell me about this spirit you've gone and got yourself attached to." She must have sensed my surprise. "Put your eyes back in your head, *chérie*. I might not see what you see, but I have other senses working overtime."

"It's just that I've never met anyone else who was aware of ghosts."

"Some magic is written down in spell books and needs to be recited in precisely the right way with the correct ingredients in just the right amounts. My magic is different than that. It's a feeling, a vibration, a flow that comes from the Almighty. That's how I know it's good and right. I can feel evil, but then I think most people can. Don't you?"

"I do." I figured I might as well tell her everything. "Cedric LeBlanc is his name." I glanced over at Cedric who'd made himself comfortable on the settee. "He's sitting right there."

"Mr. LeBlanc, welcome to my home." She seemed to look right at him, then turned back to me. "And my grandson brought you here so I could help him move on?"

"Oh. I'm not really sure why he brought me here except maybe you'd tell him if he should believe me. I'm not sure he's comfortable with the idea of a ghost helping solve his own murder." I glanced at Cedric who was listening eagerly.

"Is this a regular thing of yours?" Odile asked. "Seeing ghosts?"

"It happens more often than I'd like. A few months ago, George and Pearl started following me around practically everywhere. They came along on our trip."

"Interesting." She waited for me to continue.

"For some reason, I only see ghosts who need help of some sort. I've managed to solve a couple of murders for ghosts who found me. It's almost like I'm a private investigator for the ghostly realm. They won't leave me alone until they find out who killed them. I think I'm stuck with Cedric until his murder is solved."

The room became nearly silent as the outdoor noises faded away. I could almost hear my heart beating. Odile's eyes were closed so I sat as still as I could and waited.

She finally spoke, barely above a whisper. "He knows who done him in. He needs you to help him accept it. That's your true purpose."

"My purpose?"

"Yes." She opened her eyes and smiled. "That and living life to the fullest. I believe that's everyone's purpose. That and being kind."

Her words calmed me, as if I'd been waiting for someone to tell me that living a good life was enough of a purpose.

"I'm sure you've helped others accept what is. Without acceptance, we get stuck. Like me. When my husband died back in 2003, I couldn't accept it. He was taken from me suddenly. I wasn't ready to let him go. It was a dark time."

Cedric spoke up. "He's still here. Can't you see him?"

A handsome man in a three-piece suit shimmered into view behind her. He caught me looking at him and held a finger up to his mouth and gave his head a quick shake.

"Wouldn't it be nice if he was still here?" I asked. "Hovering around, waiting until you were ready to join him?"

She chuckled. "Sometimes I think I can feel his presence. I say, Raymond, is that you? But I don't get an answer." She sighed. "And I suppose that's my answer. He's moved on, and I know he'd want me to do the same and live what life I've got left. I know we'll be together someday, and for now, I've got my grandkids to keep me busy."

I nodded at the man, who smiled gratefully before he faded away again.

Odile leaned forward in her chair. "Back to Mr. Cedric LeBlanc, what can I do to help?"

"I'm not sure." I didn't see how an elderly woman could help solve a murder, but what did I have to lose? "He wants me to find out who killed him, but he honestly hasn't been a whole lot of help." I glanced over at Cedric. "No offense."

"That's because the person responsible for his passing is someone he doesn't want to believe would want to hurt him. It's hard to accept that someone you love would betray you. And murder is the ultimate betrayal."

"Of course. Sally," I said, just as Azemar returned to the room.

Cedric jumped out of his chair. "No, I've told you before. She wouldn't hurt a fly."

I repeated his words for Azemar and his grand-mother's benefit. "Sally has an alibi." I felt deflated. "But Detective, you never told me where she was or who she was with the night Cedric was murdered."

Azemar gave me a funny look. "He's here? Right now?"

I gestured to the settee where Cedric sat again, sulking. "Right there."

"Uh huh." Azemar stared at the settee then turned back to me. "Maybe he doesn't want to hear what Sally's alibi is."

Cedric took in a breath and let it out slowly. Or at least he appeared to, since ghosts didn't breathe. "I can take whatever the boy detective has to say."

It took a lot to keep from laughing at that. "He says he can take it."

"Sally and Jimmy Joe were together that night." He paused, then added, "All night."

Cedric scowled. "Doin' what? Talking?"

For Cedric's benefit, I asked, "When you say they were together, you mean…?"

Azemar nodded. "According to Sally, she and Cedric had been on a break. I think that's how she put it. And, according to her, she had, um, needs. And Jimmy Joe wasn't good for much of anything, also according to her, but he was good at, um…"

"I get the picture." Cedric blinked back tears. "But that doesn't mean she killed me."

Cedric had a thick skull, that was for sure, but Odile was right. He needed to accept the truth.

"If Sally killed Cedric," I said, "maybe Jimmy Joe figured it out. Or maybe they were both involved, which would explain why they gave each other an alibi."

"And if that's the case, I'd lay odds that she killed Jimmy Joe too," Azemar said. "Maybe she was afraid he'd spill the beans."

"Jimmy Joe liked his beer," I said. "After a few or ten, he might start to blab. I suppose Sally couldn't risk it."

Cedric sat with his face in his hands, and I could tell by the way his body shook that he was sobbing.

"I'm so sorry, Cedric."

Cedric dropped his hands to his lap and a strange look came over him, a mixture of sadness and hopelessness. "There's nothing for me here anymore."

As I watched him fade, I whispered, "Goodbye, Cedric. Have a happy, restful afterlife." I blinked back a tear. "It was nice knowing you."

A huge weight lifted from my body and a peaceful feeling enveloped me. "You were right," I told Odile. "He needed to accept the truth before he could move on. He's gone now."

"I felt him leave." She looked from me to her grandson. "The air feels lighter in here, doesn't it?"

Azemar shrugged. "If you say so."

CHAPTER 22

*A*fter thanking Odile for her hospitality, I accepted Azemar's offer to walk me back to the hotel. We passed a park surrounded by magnificent oak trees which he pointed out as Elysian Fields Park.

"It's hard to believe we're so close to the French Quarter," I said. "This part of the city has such a different feel to it."

"The city is changing, but the locals are intent on preserving our history and the flavor of the neighborhoods."

"Where are we?" I didn't recognize anything around us. "We're close to my hotel, aren't we?"

He pointed at the next street. "That's Royal Street."

"Oh, good. Now I know where we are." At the corner, I looked left and right. "Which direction is it?"

He chuckled and gestured to the right.

Small Creole cottages, many of them painted in bright oranges and greens, and others in pastel shades, gave way to lovely big houses with more than one address on the front, obviously converted to multi-family housing, some with wood siding and big front porches and others red brick with wrought iron railings.

The street curved, and after a few more blocks we crossed Esplanade Avenue, a wide boulevard with a row of oak trees down the center median.

"Now you're back in the French Quarter," Azemar said. "See those tall buildings in the distance? That's the business district."

"Are you going to arrest Sally?" I asked. "Or do you have to convince your partner first?"

His face fell. "First, we need some hard evidence. Anything that would tie her to his house the night of the murder. There aren't any witnesses, since everyone on the street was asleep at the time."

"What about doorbell cameras?"

"We already went down that route. The few cameras on that street are motion sensitive and didn't pick up anything, so no video."

"What about at Jimmy Joe's?" I thought about the nosy neighbor. "Remember the nosy woman next door? Maybe she was used to seeing Sally at Jimmy Joe's house and didn't think anything of it, so she didn't say anything."

He was quiet as we walked, then said, "You might be onto something. I'll go talk to her as soon as I drop you off."

"I can find my way back from here, Detective."

He stopped and shook my hand. "Thanks for your help, Ms. May."

"Please call me April."

"Thank you, April." He smiled. "And you can call me Detective Azemar."

I nodded knowingly. "Your first name is that embarrassing, huh? That's okay. I'm sure I can look it up on the internet."

He grimaced and sucked in a breath before he answered. "Horace."

It took some effort, but I managed to not laugh. "Nice to meet you, Horace. And thank you for taking me to meet your grandmother. I hope you'll understand it's nothing personal when I say I hope I never see you again."

I walked past the shop that Cedric had insisted we visit that first day, then doubled back. What harm would it do to pop in and see if Madame Morgana was in?

This time, no one sat at the front counter. Maybe they were short staffed. I walked past voodoo dolls, shrunken heads and potions with labels claiming they could cure your ills or fix your love life and into the equally cramped back area.

A tall, angular woman with dark frizzy hair stood with her back to me in the doorway of a small room. It didn't look much bigger than a closet.

Softly, so I didn't startle her, I said, "Excuse me."

She yelped and swung around to face me. A

stripe of white hair had escaped from a clip she'd used to tame her hair.

"I'm so sorry," I said. "I didn't mean to startle you. I'm looking for Madame Morgana."

"I am," she said in a low dramatic voice, "Madame Morgana."

CHAPTER 23

ossing one of the colorful shawls she wore over her shoulders, she ushered me into the small, cluttered room and gestured to a chair. I sat and watched as she fluttered around the tiny space like a moth that didn't know where to land, moving things around with no purpose I could see.

Finally, she snatched yet another a fringed shawl from the back of a chair, threw it around her shoulders, and collapsed into an overstuffed purple velveteen chair. It had been elegant once, I had no doubt, but now it showed wear around the edges.

With a swipe of her arm, she pushed everything off the table and into a wooden box. "My doom box."

I raised my eyebrows. "Doom?"

The corners of her lips turned up a tiny bit. "Don't organize. Only move."

"Don't..." I tried to make sense of what she'd

said. "Oh! D-O-O-M. I have several doom boxes myself at home."

"Where is home?" she asked, as she dug through another box. She retrieved a fat candle and set it on a tray.

"Northern California. A little town called Serenity Cove about an hour and a half north of the Bay Area. San Francisco," I added, in case she didn't know what I meant by the Bay Area.

She lit the candle and stared at it for what felt like a long time. I waited, not wanting to interrupt her thoughts. Finally, she pulled out a deck of tarot cards and laid three in a row in front of her.

She turned to me and spoke in a soft, somewhat dramatic voice. "You have come a long way to find your purpose."

"Um, actually, I'm on vacation. I brought my assistant to New Orleans for a quick trip. It's her first time out of California."

She looked at me, first in the eyes then the rest of my face, finally traveling to my hands and feet. What was she looking for?

"Why did you seek me out?" she asked.

"A friend suggested I come see you. We stopped by the other day, but you weren't in. He thought you could help us solve a..." I almost said "murder," but stopped myself. "Solve a problem. But now it's solved so I'm not sure why I came in. I saw the sign and just thought I'd..." I'd what? Why had I come into the shop? "I guess I'm not really sure, but Cedric thought—"

"Cedric?" Her eyes widened. She reached out and grabbed my arm—gently, but it still startled me. "Does he still have the talisman?"

My heart nearly stopped beating. "You know about the talisman?"

"Of course, I know about the talisman. I know it is cursed. I knew it the moment I saw it, but Cedric didn't believe me. Where is Cedric now? I must speak with him."

There didn't seem much reason not to tell her the truth. "He's dead. He died Monday night, or possibly the early hours of Tuesday morning."

She didn't seem surprised or upset about Cedric's death. "And the talisman?"

Now it was my turn to search her face for clues, but I didn't see signs of deception. Just curiosity.

"I don't know where the talisman is at the moment. I think his girlfriend Sally has it." I assumed she took it from Jimmy Joe's house when she killed him.

For another long moment, she stared into the candle's flame before turning back to me. "We must find it."

"We?" When she nodded eagerly, I asked, "You mean you and me?"

"Yes, of course. The talisman must be decursed if possible, before anyone else dies. If it can't be decursed, it must be destroyed."

Was decursed even a word? "Don't you think that's a little dramatic? A piece of jewelry isn't responsible for anyone's death."

"Is that so?" She raised her left eyebrow nearly a half an inch. "There has already been one death, *chérie*."

I swallowed hard. "Two."

She grabbed my arm again. "Who else has died?"

I yanked my arm away from her surprisingly strong grasp. "Stop doing that, and I'll tell you." I rubbed my arm which probably would have a colorful bruise in a day or so. "His friend Jimmy Joe is dead, probably murdered by the same person who killed Cedric. I can't be sure he had the talisman when he died, but he did have it earlier that day."

She leaned closer. "And who killed Cedric and Jimmy…"

"Jimmy Joe." I shrugged. "I don't have any proof."

She lifted her chin and closed her eyes. "But you have a strong feeling, I can see it in your aura." She opened her eyes again. "Tell me what you know, and I will help you."

I sighed, regretting coming to see this strange woman. "I told the police detective everything I know. He'll take it from here." I didn't want to get involved, or rather, I wanted to get uninvolved. Cedric's and Jimmy Joe's murders were no longer my responsibility, if they ever were.

She slumped back into her chair and stared at the ceiling. In a soft voice, she said, "You do not understand your purpose."

I followed her gaze, but there was nothing but cracked plaster overhead. "I don't have a purpose other than serving tea, scones, and dainty little sandwiches at my tearoom in California. I'm not some detective solving crimes for ghosts."

Her eyes widened.

I tried to take it back although I knew it was too late. "I mean ghosts, figuratively. Like the ghosts of the past."

She folded her arms over her chest and gave me a sly grin. Her thick southern accent disappeared along with her fake Madame Morgana persona. The next words came out in a Valley Girl accent, which was not what I expected.

"No freaking way."

"What happened to your accent?"

"You can see ghosts."

"Where are you from?" I asked, not wanting to admit she was right.

"I grew up in Sherman Oaks. Actually, Van Nuys, but who wants to be from Van Nuys? But never mind me, tell me about the ghosts."

After considering my options, I decided to tell her everything, or at least the short version starting with Fanny and Chef Emile Toussaint and ending in Cedric LeBlanc, Jimmy Joe, and their murders.

"It seems I can only see ghost who need me to solve their murders, but I refuse to accept that as my purpose. My scones make people happy. Isn't that enough?"

She leaned forward again and took my hand in

hers. I half expected her to turn it over and read my palm.

Instead, she said, "You didn't solve Fanny's murder. And you haven't solved Cedric's murder either."

"Oh, yes, I have. It was his girlfriend, Sally. That's why Cedric went off to heaven or wherever spirits go after they accept they need to move on."

"Exactly," she said, giving my hand a gentle squeeze before letting it go. "He moved on because you helped him accept his death. It was a lack of acceptance keeping him here, not because he needed his murder solved. It might be best that he doesn't know who killed him."

That made no sense, but I'd worry about that later. I stood and pulled out my wallet. "Thanks so much for your time. How much do I owe you?"

"The only thing you owe me is helping me find that talisman so I can remove the curse from it." Leaping to her feet, she began removing her shawls one by one, throwing them on the chair. She froze at the sound of a knock.

"Did anyone follow you here?" she asked.

What an odd question. "The only person who's been following me lately is one of the police detectives, but I'm pretty sure he's got better things to do at the moment."

She called out in her dramatic Madame Morgana voice. "Who is it?"

The door opened, and there stood Nadine, Cedric's sister.

She started when she saw me. "Hello, April. What are you doing here? Oh, that musta sounded rude. I'm just surprised is all."

"Me, too."

We stood awkwardly for a few seconds before Madame Morgana cleared her throat.

"Oh, right," I said. "Madame Morgana, this is Nadine, Cedric's sister."

Nadine smiled and reached out her hand. "Pleased to meet you, ma'am. My brother Cedric told me so much about you."

"Really?" I asked, but the two women ignored me.

Morgana, or whatever her real name was, had fully returned to her woo-woo ways and voice. "And you have come seeking answers." She pulled the shawls off the chair and tossed them into the corner, pushing the chair toward Nadine, who took the offered seat.

"Thank you kindly."

Morgana shot me a look, then glanced at the chair I'd just risen from. I wasn't sure what she was trying to communicate, but when I sat back down, she seemed relieved. She plopped back down into her velveteen chair, and the three of us sat in the tiny room, our knees nearly touching.

Nadine glanced at me, then back to Morgana and lowered her voice. "I thought perhaps we could speak alone."

"What do you have to say to Madame Morgana

that you don't want me to hear?" I smiled, hoping it didn't sound confrontational.

"Oh, goodness!" She laughed and brushed off my question with a wave of her hand. "It's not that, but surely you have somewhere else to be. This could take some time."

I made a show of checking the time on my phone. "I'm not meeting Jennifer for another hour," I fibbed, "so I can stick around, but only if you don't mind."

"Oh heavens no." She appeared to be undecided about what to do. Did she not trust me?

Madame Morgana and I sat in silence, waiting for Nadine to make the first move. We didn't have to wait long.

She reached into her purse to retrieve something.

I may have gasped at the sight of the talisman, but if so, Nadine didn't seem to notice. She held the pendant in her open palm, the chain hanging down, swinging slowly like a pendulum.

"I've only seen it in pictures." I reached out my hand. "May I get a closer look?"

"Don't touch it!" Morgana warned and I snatched my hand away.

Nadine sounded offended. "Why not?"

Instead of answering, Morgana asked the question I wanted to know. "Where did you get it?"

Nadine clasped the talisman to her breast. "It belonged to my dear brother, Cedric. It's one of the few things I have to remember him by."

"He gave it to you?" I asked, keeping my voice light. "I thought it was stolen the night he died."

"What made you think that?" Nadine asked innocently. "He had told me he wanted me to have it, so when I found it in his house, I took it. I wanted to make sure it was safe. For all I knew, he'd given Sally a key to his place, and I wanted to make sure she didn't take anything else." She turned to Morgana. "I'm almost sure she's the one who killed him, but the police won't listen to me. If it wasn't for April..." She reached for my hand. "You do believe me, don't you?"

At that moment, I didn't know who or what to believe, but I kept that to myself and took her hand. "Of course I believe you. In fact, I just told Detective Azemar that he needs to find the evidence to arrest Sally for Cedric and Jimmy Joe's murder."

She seemed confused for a moment, then nodded. "Of course. She killed Jimmy Joe. They must have been in on it together. Or maybe he knew too much."

I stared at her other hand, still clasping the talisman. How had Nadine really gained possession of it?

CHAPTER 24

My phone buzzed with a text from Jennifer who was, in her words, "starving." I replied, "I'm on my way."

I stood to leave. "Thank you for the visit, Madam Morgana. Do you believe you can lift the curse from the talisman?"

"Curse?" Nadine's hand flew open, and the talisman dropped to the floor.

Morgana grabbed a pen and lifted the talisman by its chain and set it on the desk. "I will do my best."

I said goodbye to Nadine and Madame Morgana and made my way back to the front of the shop. After typing a text message to Detective Azemar about Nadine and the talisman, I deleted it. It didn't seem to make much sense. Besides, the detective was perfectly capable of solving the murders without my help.

Maybe Nadine took it from Jimmy Joe's house

and was afraid she'd be accused of theft. Or maybe she'd seen Jimmy Joe earlier that day and he'd given it to her, knowing her brother would want her to have it.

For all I knew, she'd given it to Jimmy Joe to find out how much it was worth. That was as plausible a theory as any.

As I stepped onto the street, the French Quarter seemed to have come alive. Music spilled from every corner, from rock music spilling out from a neon-signed club to the rhythmic strum of a lone guitarist on the corner of Royal Street.

Donkeys pulling carriages clopped past. The sky looked heavy with the promise of more rain, the thick clouds tinged with the fading pinks and purples of twilight. Even the sidewalks seemed to hum with the echoes of centuries of laughter, music, and whispers embedded in every brick and stone.

There wasn't any place in the world like the French Quarter and no city like New Orleans. No wonder people had been falling in love with the Big Easy for generations.

AFTER FRESHENING UP QUICKLY, SO JENNIFER DIDN'T pass out from hunger, I knocked on her door. She threw it open, looking fresh as the daisies printed on her dress.

"There's a hole in the wall a block or two from

here on my list. I don't think I'm up for a lot of walking this evening."

"Same. I'm exhausted," Jennifer said, showing no sign of fatigue.

Everything at dinner make me think of Cedric, from the boudin balls we ordered for an appetizer to the server's accent. I could have sworn I heard someone call their friend a "couyon."

"Tell me about your visit with the detective's grandmother."

I smiled, remembering her kindness and warmth. I filled her in on our conversation, and her opinions about magic.

"Do you think that's why you can see ghosts?" Jennifer asked. "Do you have magic powers?"

I chuckled. "If so, I'm really mad I didn't get a letter when I turned thirteen. But you know how I feel about magic. It's everywhere."

She smiled and nodded. "I think so too."

"Back to reality tomorrow," I reminded her. "The tearoom is going to be slow for the next couple of months, but I don't mind at all. I'm kind of worn out from the busy summer months." And from the trip, but I wasn't going to say that out loud. I hated to admit that age had slowed me down.

"Oh." Jennifer clapped her hands together excitedly. "We can have a Halloween event."

"The last time we had a Halloween event, someone was murdered, remember?"

Jennifer's mouth turned down in a pout. "But that had nothing to do with the event. Are you going to change how you run the tearoom every time there's a mishap?"

"I don't think death is considered a mishap."

"You know what I mean. We should do themed spooky teas the last two weekends in October, and if it goes over well, we can extend it next year. What do you say?"

Her eagerness won me over. "Sure, why not. Besides, it would be fun to come up with some new themed recipes. I saw a recipe once for mummy sausage rolls."

"I love your sausage rolls. Or how about chocolate coffin eclairs?"

I grinned. "I like it." Looking around the room at the eclectic decor, I sighed. "I love New Orleans, but I'll be glad to get home."

"It's been fun, but I'd love to come back sometime when there isn't a murder to solve. Do you think solving murders is your purpose—the reason you can see ghosts?"

I stared at my hand, remembering how Odile had held it gently in hers. "Azemar's grandmother said my purpose is to live life to the fullest and be kind whenever possible. I think she might be onto something."

"I wish I'd gone along to meet her."

"Me too. Too bad we leave tomorrow. She has this hound dog that must be a hundred and fifty in dog years. His ears were so long they almost touched the ground."

"Darn it. I love dogs. Did you know you can own a hedgehog in Louisiana?"

I laughed. "You need to warn me if you're going to change subjects that fast. I could get whiplash."

Her brows knit together. "We were talking about pets. Hedgehogs can be pets, at least here. Not in California, though. I wonder why?"

"You're not moving out of state, so you can have a hedgehog, I hope." I was half kidding, but having her own hedgehog might be important to her for all I knew, although she'd never mentioned it before.

"Not anytime soon. I need to get enough credits to transfer to a university."

The server appeared and offered dessert menus. "I highly recommend the bread pudding souffle with whiskey sauce. It's the specialty of the house."

Jennifer raised her eyebrows. "Do you want to share one?"

"Our last night in New Orleans? I think we should share two desserts. You know, in case we don't care for one of them then we won't be disappointed."

"I assure you," the server said, "That will not happen."

I held up a hand. "I'm sure it won't." I ordered the bread pudding souffle and a pecan pie a la mode along with another French 75. "I could get used to living like this."

As we strolled back to the hotel, Jennifer asked. "Are you done for the evening?" The eagerness in her voice told me she wasn't ready to call it a night.

"Where should we go?" I asked.

"Can we…?" She hesitated, then blurted out, "I'd love some red beans and rice."

I laughed. "How can you possibly eat anything after everything we just ate?" And not gain an ounce by the looks of her. Oh, to have a young metabolism again.

"It might be my last chance."

I had two words for her. "Room service."

Jennifer went to her room to change into comfy clothes. While I was perusing the room service menu, Pearl made an appearance.

"How've you been enjoying the local speakeasies?" I asked.

"Speakeasies! You think I've been having fun while there's a murderer running around free as a jailbird?"

"Well, yes."

"I've been watching Sally, waiting for her to trip up and give herself away. But you know what? That ole girl's eyes are as red as a ripe tomato from all the crying she'd been doin'. And ain't nobody around. Why's she crying if she's not sad?"

"Guilt?" I suggested.

Pearl pursed her lips in a pout. "I'm not buying what you're selling. I don't think she killed Cedric or Jimmy Joe. Especially Jimmy Joe. Them two was as thick as thieves."

"That's not what you said yesterday." I grumbled. I felt like a ball in a pinball machine getting banged back and forth. "I wish you would make up your mind."

Pearl put a hand on her hip. "I did make up my mind. I just changed it, that's all."

"If Sally didn't kill Cedric and Jimmy Joe, then who did?" I felt a headache coming on.

George sat with his feet resting on the edge of the bed. He jerked his chin in my direction. "I thought you said Jimmy Joe killed Cedric. I wish *you'd* make up your mind." Under his breath, he added, "Women."

"Yeah." Pearl sashayed over to me and poked a finger at my chest. "How come you can change your mind, but I can't?"

"Because Jimmy Joe is dead."

"He is now," George said. "But he was alive when Cedric died, now wasn't he?"

"Yeah." Pearl hurried over to her beau and sat on the arm of his chair. "George is right."

I sat on the edge of the bed and considered what they said. I had to admit they had a point. "But if Jimmy Joe killed Cedric, then who killed Jimmy Joe? And why?"

George wrapped an arm around Pearl's waist. "We gotta figure out everything for you?"

Pearl leaned down and started kissing George as he began to run his hands over her body. The whole thing made me uncomfortable.

I turned my back to them. "Get a room. And by that, I mean your own room, not mine."

When I peeked over my shoulder to check, they were gone.

How were the police going to figure out if Sally killed Cedric or not? After all, her alibi partner was dead. I pulled out my phone to send Azemar a text to update him on what I'd learned.

But what had I actually learned? Sally being really sad about Cedric and Jimmy Joe's deaths didn't prove she was innocent.

The room seemed empty without any of the ghosts. I almost missed Cedric.

"Cedric, what if I got it wrong?" I said to the empty room. "What if you spend eternity thinking Sally killed you and she didn't?"

The one consoling thought I had was that Azemar would get to the truth. And Bowman. He must have been a good detective, or he'd never have gotten promoted to lead detective. He probably had too many cases to spend all his time on one middle-aged guy in Uptown.

I hoped he'd learn not to jump to conclusions so quickly, but I knew people didn't change, at least not most people.

Like Nadine. She'd been fiercely loyal as a kid, willing to do anything to protect her brother. And if she couldn't protect him, how far would she be willing to go to get revenge on someone who'd killed Cedric?

CHAPTER 25

My phone buzzed with a text from Nadine.

You're leaving tomorrow?

I stared at the phone for several seconds before typing my response.

First thing in the AM.

As I waited for the next text, I nearly nodded off in my chair. I felt drained from the excitement and drama of the last few days, as well as being hot and sticky from the heat and humidity of New Orleans. Maybe a cool shower would revive me.

After showering and dressing, I checked the phone again, but no new texts. Should I text her again? And say what? She'd see right through any platitudes—sorry I couldn't help more, sorry you still don't know who killed your brother, sorry, sorry, sorry.

What did Nadine expect from me? Surely, she

didn't think I could do what trained homicide detectives couldn't.

Someone tapped on the door lightly. I went to let Jennifer in, but instead Nadine stood in the hallway.

"May I come in?" she asked.

"I was just getting ready to go out," I fibbed.

"I won't take up much of your time, I promise."

I stepped aside to let her enter and gestured to one of the chairs. Perched on the edge of the bed, I waited to hear the reason for her visit.

She finally spoke. "I was convinced that Sally killed my brother."

"So was I," I said. "Well, first I thought Sally, then I was sure it was Jimmy Joe since he had the talisman. Now I figure it must have been Sally, since Sally and Jimmy Joe were each other's alibis."

"What makes you think Jimmy Joe had the talisman?"

Oops. Maybe I shouldn't have mentioned that. "He took it to a pawn shop."

"The police shared that information with you? They never told me."

"It's more like I shared the information with the police," I said. "Believe me, they're not telling me any more than they're telling you. Probably less, since you're his sister."

"That's why you looked so surprised when you saw it. You knew I'd gotten it from Jimmy Joe."

"What I can't figure out is how Jimmy Joe got it. Cedric doesn't remember giving it to Jimmy Joe." I caught my slip of the tongue. "I mean, Cedric didn't tell me he gave it away. But I don't see how else Jimmy Joe could have gotten it."

"He could have taken it after he killed Cedric."

Her words caught me off guard and I didn't know what to say at first. "You think Jimmy Joe killed your brother?" When she nodded, I asked, "But then who killed Jimmy Joe?"

She paused long enough for the truth to hit me.

"I'd like to know that too," she said, "but if he killed my brother, then I'm not shedding any tears over him."

If she saw the suspicion in my eyes, she didn't let it show. Nadine was as cool as a New Orleans breeze in February.

"The people Jimmy Joe associated with were not exactly the cream of society. Maybe he and that lowlife Marcel had a falling out or something."

"Maurice," I corrected her. "And you have a point. I'm pretty sure Maurice is a fence dealing in stolen merchandise."

Her lips curled in a smile. "I always knew he was the criminal sort."

In an effort to change the subject, I asked, "What are you planning to do with Cedric's house? Do you think you'll move back to New Orleans?"

She stared at the carpet before replying. "There are too many bad memories here. I'll find someone to fix it up and then sell it. Or maybe rent it. The rental market is quite strong these days."

We sat in silence while I considered how to get her to leave. I was itching to call Detective Azemar.

"Is there anything else you wanted to talk to me about?" I asked.

She looked me straight in the eye and I gave her a warm smile that I hoped she would find reassuring.

She stood. "Thanks for your time, April May."

"Take care, Nadine."

I opened the door and held it open for her.

She stopped in the doorway and said, "I suppose you think I'm a horrible person for having no pity for Jimmy Joe."

"Not at all," I said. "If someone killed my brother, I don't think I'd be sad about their death."

She smiled half-heartedly. "I hope you never are faced with that situation."

Closing the door behind her, I leaned against it and tried to calm my nerves. I'd had suspicions about who killed Cedric and Jimmy Joe, but until moments ago, I'd thought they were the same person.

CHAPTER 26

This time when someone tapped on the door, I checked the peephole. When I saw Jennifer's smiling face, relief washed over me. I pulled the door open a crack.

"Anyone else out there?" I asked.

Her smile faded. "No…"

Opening the door wider, I pulled her into the room. "Nadine was just here."

"Oh." She got a worried look on her face. "April, what's going on?"

"I need a drink," I said, grabbing my purse.

Jennifer waited patiently as we waited for the elevator, then made our way to the lobby. I beelined to the lobby bar where we found a small table in the corner.

I ordered a Sazerac, saying, "It's our last chance for authentic New Orleans cocktails."

Jennifer requested a French 75, then, when the server left, said, "Okay, now tell me what's up with

Nadine. You looked like you'd seen a ghost." She frowned. "Wrong comparison in your case. You looked like you'd had a fright."

"When I went to see Madame Morgana earlier today, Nadine had the talisman."

"I thought Jimmy Joe had it."

"He did. I'm sure of it."

"Jimmy Joe gave it to Nadine?"

"That's what she says now. But at Madame Morgana's, she said Cedric had given it to her."

"She lied."

The server set the drinks in front of us, and I drank half of mine in one gulp.

Jennifer daintily sipped her champagne cocktail. "Is it a big deal that she lied? Maybe she didn't want you to know she'd talked to Jimmy Joe."

"Exactly. And why wouldn't she want us to know that she'd seen Jimmy Joe on the day he was murdered?"

She gasped. "You think Nadine is the murderer? You think she killed her own brother?"

I shook my head. "No. I think she killed her brother's murderer."

Jennifer wrinkled her brow in confusion, but as I sipped the rest of my drink, her expression changed.

"Jimmy Joe killed Cedric," she said in a whisper. "And then…"

"Nadine killed Jimmy Joe."

Pearl shimmered into view next to our table, wearing a sparkly fringed dress that made a rustling noise every time she moved. "I told you Sally didn't do it."

"Yes." I gave her an indulgent smile. "Thank you for all your help solving this case."

She must have missed my sarcasm, because she nearly blushed. "Aw, it's nothing. So, what you gonna do now?"

I sighed and leaned back in my chair. "I guess I'll tell Detective Azemar what I've learned, but without any evidence, I'm not sure it will do any good."

"Is it so bad if she gets away with it?" Jennifer asked. "I mean, what she did was wrong, but he did kill her brother."

Pearl spoke in a firm voice. "Justice is mine, sayeth the Lord."

"I think it's 'Vengeance is mine.'"

"Are you sure?" Pearl asked. "I never was too good at remembering the bible."

"Justice belongs in the courts, Pearl. Besides, what if Nadine got it wrong? It's possible she killed an innocent man."

Jennifer's mouth hung open. "You think so?"

I shrugged. "It's not up to me to decide."

I stepped away from the table and called Detective Azemar. The call went to voicemail. This wasn't information that belonged in a voice mail or text, so I asked him to call me back.

When I returned to the table, I asked Jennifer if we should stick to our plans for room service or go out. "I'm feeling a bit more rested." The drink had helped, too.

"Can we go back to Napoleon House?" she asked.

"For red beans and rice?"

"They were really good there. Maybe when we get home you could make them and teach me how. I'll clean up."

"You bet. All we need is the right recipe and the right ingredients. It might take a few tries before we get it right."

"That's okay with me," she said with a grin.

We went out the back exit of the hotel and headed down Chartres Street, with Pearl strolling along and sharing stories of her time in New Orleans a hundred years earlier.

"Lotsa things haven't changed a bit," she said. "Same old buildings. Same juice joints." She eyed a group of young people in torn jeans drinking from plastic cups. "Other things have changed, and not for the better."

Azemar returned my call, and I told him what I'd learned from Nadine. "She didn't exactly confess, but…"

"Even if she had confessed to you, I doubt we could make it stick."

"Why not?"

"It would be your word against hers. And if I bring her in, I doubt she'll confess to me."

"You're saying she's going to get away with murder?" As far as murderers went, I didn't see her as a threat to society, but my keen sense of justice didn't like her going free.

"Some do, April. We do our best. And maybe she'll slip up and we'll nail her."

"Could you get a subpoena and hook me up with a wire? I can try to get her to confess while you're listening on the other end."

"You've been watching too many movies, April. In Louisiana, you can record a conversation as long as one person knows about it. But if she only hinted at what she's done, she's not about to turn around and give you a full confession now."

"I suppose not." I'd always believed that murderers always make a mistake, either in committing the crime or in covering it up. All we had to do was be there when she made her next mistake.

George appeared next to Pearl, who must have still been angry with him, since gave him a shove. Unfortunately, she shoved him right into me, or rather through me. No matter how many times a ghost made contact with me, it always creeped me out.

"Ugh," I said with a full body shiver. "Don't do that."

"Do what?" Azemar asked, still on the phone.

"Oh!" An idea had popped into my head. "Hold on, detective."

"What's wrong?" Jennifer asked. "You look like you just rubbed up against a slug."

"Pearl shoved George into me, and it gave me the willies."

Pearl laughed. "It's fun to watch, but it doesn't feel great for us either, otherwise we might do it more often just for giggles."

"Can you try on Jennifer?"

Jennifer gave me a sideways glance. "Try what?"

"Just her hand," I said, adding to Jennifer, "Would you mind terribly?"

Sucking in a breath, she said, "I'm guessing you have a good reason for asking."

"I do."

She scrunched up her face, closed her eyes, and held her hand out.

Pearl reached out and put her hand through Jennifer's. Jennifer shrieked and yanked back her hand.

"Are you okay?" I asked, regretting making the request of her.

"I'm fine." Jennifer gave me a sheepish smile. "I sort of overreacted because I didn't know what to expect. It felt like... like my hand got all squishy or something. It's hard to describe."

"Perfect." I got back on the phone and told Azemar my plan.

CHAPTER 27

*P*earl practically skipped alongside us as
we made our way back to the Vampyre
Boutique. The scent of incense wafted through the
open door.

George, meanwhile, sulked behind us, grum-
bling about wanting his girl to join him at one of the
ghostly speakeasies in town.

"There'll be time for all that later," Pearl said in a
scolding yet playful tone.

Jennifer waited outside, not willing to go back to
the hotel and wait. She promised to stay out of
sight.

Madame Morgana, once again swathed in
scarves, greeted us the moment we stepped inside
the shop. "Nadine took the bait," Morgana said, her
voice low and conspiratorial. "She should be here
any minute."

"Just do your part, and hopefully we'll have a
full confession before long."

Morgana led us to the back and her tiny, cramped room. "You can really see ghosts?" she asked me as we settled into our chairs, leaving one empty for Nadine. "I've felt them around me from time to time, but I've never actually seen them. Can you tell me who is with us here now?"

"Just the two ghosts who followed me from California." I told her about George and Pearl, intentionally leaving out the troubling part about Pearl shooting George. I preferred not to remind George about that. "I think Cedric has moved on, so I don't think he'll be making an appearance. But Nadine doesn't need to know that."

Morgana raised an eyebrow. "You think your two ghosts will make her believe he's here?"

"We could give her a little taste." A mischievous grin spread across George's face.

"Nobody needs a taste, George." How Pearl put up with George's antics was beyond me. True, he was as loyal as a sheepdog—at least one who sniffed after every girl dog.

Madame Morgana dug through a box and pulled out a dozen candles, lighting them one by one and setting them around the room. Next, she lit a stick of incense, and the pungent smell of sandal-wood soon surrounded us.

As she turned off the bright overhead light, leaving only the warm light from a lamp and the candlelight to see by, a soft tap on the door made us all hold our breaths, anticipation hanging thick in the air.

"Come in," Madame Morgana said in the low, dramatic voice she'd used before.

The door slowly creaked open and Nadine appeared, her eyes wide and her mouth dropping open. "You didn't say *she* would be here."

Morgana's eyes turned to me as if she hadn't noticed I was in the room, then spoke to Nadine. "April has a special connection to the spectral world." She paused, letting that sink in. "*And* your brother."

"What are you talking about?"

"Sit," Morgana commanded, and Nadine complied, sitting stiffly on the chair. She set her purse on her lap and waited.

"Did you know that April didn't know your brother before he died?"

Nadine's brows drew together in confusion as she stared at me. "You said you two were close. You told me he was going to show you around town." Her lips pulled down in a scowl. "You're a liar."

I took her insult in stride. "He did show me around town, Nadine, but not while he was alive." It was my turn to pause dramatically. I lowered my voice to just above a whisper. "I only met him the morning after he died."

"How could you possibly...?" Her voice trailed off as she considered the possibilities.

"I met Cedric's ghost the morning after he was murdered."

Nadine gasped. "What are the two of you trying

to pull?" Her frown lines deepened as her anger grew.

"We're not trying to 'pull' anything," Morgana said, her tone reassuring.

Nadine harrumphed and clutched her purse tightly. "You're not getting a penny out of me."

"We don't want your money, Nadine," I said, my voice gentle. "Cedric came to me to help him learn who was responsible for his death. He couldn't remember, but that's common with violent deaths."

"I see." She jerked to her feet, still clutching her purse to her chest. "I see it all now. You're a charlatan," she said, pointing at me. "And you." She turned her attention and the accusing finger on Morgana. "You must be one too, bringing me here under false pretenses. You said you could connect me with the spirit of my dear departed brother, and instead—"

"Sit," Madame Morgana said in a deep, commanding voice.

Nadine sat.

The lights dimmed, a theatrical move likely operated by a hidden switch or foot pedal, and the candles flickered casting eerie shadows on the wall. Madame Morgana began her performance, reaching out for us to take her hands.

Nadine reluctantly took my hand as Madame Morgana instructed us to close our eyes.

"Cedric LeBlanc." Her voice was deep and strong, and I half expected Cedric to appear at her command. "Speak to us." A gust of air extinguished half the candles, a very effective gimmick I thought, until I opened one eye and saw George grinning.

"Did you see that?" He could hardly have been prouder. "I can blow out candles."

I nodded to show I approved, although if George developed any more powers, I might start to worry.

Morgana's head dropped to her chest as if she'd fallen asleep. We sat in silence for several long moments. Even George and Pearl were quiet, seemingly mesmerized by what was going on.

Without warning, Morgana sat up straight with her eyes wide open. "I'm here. Nadine, Nadine…"

Nadine appeared unconvinced. In a bland voice, she answered. "Yes, I'm here."

"Why'd you do it, No-no?"

I'd shared the nickname with Morgana before we arrived along with a few other details I hoped Nadine would find convincing.

At the sound of Cedric's pet name for her, her hand tightened on mine, and she sucked in a breath. She brushed it off and mumbled, "Lucky guess."

Morgana continued, repeating words I'd remembered Cedric saying. "Why'd you call me a *couyon*? I got as much sense as the next guy."

Nadine's eyes widened, but she stayed silent, her breath steady.

"I know you love me, No-no." The voice was low and mournful. "But you shouldn't have done it."

Nadine squirmed in her chair as we all waited for her response. "Done what?"

"You shouldn't have killed my friend."

She jerked her hands back from both of us. "What are you talking about?"

"Jimmy Joe was my friend." Morgana was so convincing, I almost thought it was Cedric speaking. Her voice became stronger along with the accent. "You killed Jimmy Joe."

She leapt to her feet, her purse dropping to the floor. "If he was your friend, then why'd he kill you? Huh? Tell me that?" Glancing over at me, she pressed her lips together tightly and sat back down. "I don't believe Cedric is here. Cedric wouldn't put me through this. Cedric knew I always looked after him."

"I do know," Cedric, or rather Madame Morgana said. She slowly blinked her eyes as if coming out of a trance and straightened in her seat, throwing her shoulders back. "Cedric would like to give you one last hug."

Nadine's eyes narrowed. "But he can't, can he? He can't hug me or anyone else. Because he's dead. Because Jimmy Joe killed him. And you want me to be sorry Jimmy Joe is dead? Well, I'm not sorry. I'd give anything for one more hug from Cedric, but he's—" Her voice caught. "He's gone."

Listening to her grief, I began to feel sorry for her.

I nodded to George, who seemed confused about what I was asking him to do even though we'd discussed it. I jerked my head in her direction.

"Oh right." He stepped over to Nadine, leaned down, and put his arms around her gently. Nadine flinched, gasped, then began to sob as she felt the icy, eerie feeling of ghostly arms.

She'd come so close to confessing, but she hadn't said anything that couldn't be explained away. How could we get her to admit what she'd done?

As Nadine continued to sob, I glanced at the woman slumped in her chair and whispered, "You did great." She didn't seem to hear me. "Madame Morgana?" I reached out and gently shook her arm.

Her head jerked up and her eyes rolled back in her head, something I'd only seen in movies. "Y'all got the wrong person." Her accent had changed but sounded familiar somehow.

Had she come up with another plan on her own to coax a confession out of Nadine? I didn't see what more we could do. "Madame Morgana, you can—"

Her voice interrupted me. "Ah was there that night, sure, but ah left when Sally showed up. Me and Cedric been fightin' over her, and he was angry as a hornet."

Nadine stared at her with her mouth hanging open. George and Pearl watched intently, seemingly transfixed. I knew that accent—a slow drawl spoken like a man who had all day to say what he wanted to say.

In a shaky voice, I asked, "Jimmy Joe?"

"Cedric said to me, he said JJ—let me talk to my gal. Alone. He said it like he owned her, ya know? My gal. I figured if anyone could get him to cool down it was her. So, I left."

The hairs on my arm stood on end. "Then what happened, JJ?" I was now convinced Morgana really was channeling his spirit. How else could she have known the details of the night he died?

"I went on home. Next thing, Sally's pounding on my door. She says there was an accident and we better tell the police we'd been together all night. Well… Sally had a way of convincing me of things I didn't always want to be convinced about."

The truth hit me, and before I could stop myself, I said, "Sally killed Cedric."

"No!" Nadine sat up straight and jabbed a finger at Madam Morgana. "Jimmy Joe killed my brother. I *know* he did."

"No, ma'am. Ah woulda never hurt Cedric. Ah suppose, I sorta did by messin' with his girl, but kill him? Ah coulda never done anything like that. But Sally? Sally ain't got a pea pod of caring for nobody but herself."

We were all silent for a very long moment until Madame Morgana, or rather Jimmy Joe's slow, lazy voice said, "Ah forgive you, Nadine."

"Forgive me? For what? For killing you, Jimmy Joe? I did it, and I'm not sorry. I don't care what you say. It was you who killed my brother. It had to be you. If it wasn't you, then…" Her voice trailed off as she buried her face in her hands, sobs racking her body.

Madame Morgana collapsed in her chair, and I rushed to help her. Her eyes fluttered opened and she looked around the room until her gaze finally rested on me.

She blinked a few times. "What happened?"

"I didn't know you could actually channel spirits. Jimmy Joe was here and got Nadine to confess to his murder."

"It happens from time to time," she admitted. "Darned unpredictable, though."

"You!" Nadine jumped to her feet. "You tricked me. Cedric was never here."

"He was here." I left out the part that he wasn't the one who'd hugged her. That would be my little secret.

She stared at us, her face red and blotchy, before she announced, "I'm outta here." Throwing open the door, she ran straight into Detective Azemar.

CHAPTER 28

he flight home was uneventful, thanks to George and Pearl missing the flight. They must have been enjoying New Orleans too much to get up early and fly back with me and Jennifer.

As we landed back in California and I checked my messages, Jennifer asked if there was any news from Detective Azemar.

"Not a word. But I have no doubt he'll find a way to nail Sally for Cedric's murder. I can just imagine him turning up every time she turns around, the way he did to me the last few days."

"And still no sign of George and Pearl?"

"None." I felt a twinge at the thought I might not see the two ghostly troublemakers again, but who knew what the future held?

On the drive to Serenity Cove, Jennifer and I talked about what we were going to do once we got home.

Jennifer went first. "I'm going to sleep for fourteen hours."

"I'm going to try making beignets."

"I'm going to make café au lait to go with the beignets."

"Perfect," I said. "I'm going to tell everyone I care about that I love them. Starting with you. You're like the daughter I never had and I'm so grateful you came to work for me."

"I love you too, almost-mom."

After sniffing back a tear, I turned on the radio while Jennifer checked her phone. Soon, the turnoff to Serenity Cove appeared. We'd be home in twenty minutes.

Home. How nice that sounded.

$\mathcal{A}$s we entered the city limits of Serenity Cove, I rolled down my window to breathe in the salty sea air. Soon, the ocean appeared ahead, a sight I never got tired of seeing. The sun was just dipping below the horizon, turning the sky into a masterpiece of pinks, oranges, and purples. I turned onto our street, surprised by all the parked cars, unusual for a Friday evening.

"Looks like a lot of people decided to come watch the sun set tonight," I said as I pulled into the driveway.

"Maybe," Jennifer said noncommittally. "But I've never seen so many during the off season."

"Why else would there be so many cars?" I asked, but she didn't answer.

It wasn't until we reached the front porch steps, bags in tow, that I began to consider an alternate explanation. It sounded like a party inside.

"Irma." I set my jaw, ready for anything but

promising myself not to get mad until I knew the whole story. It wouldn't be the first time she'd taken a mile when I'd given an inch.

As I reached for the door, it swung open and two women emerged.

"You're too late," one of them said. "But maybe you can make a reservation for the next class."

"What class?" I asked.

"You're not here for the cooking class?" the other woman asked, eyeing our suitcases.

The first woman gushed. "It's so much more than just a cooking class. Irma says we need to 'rediscover the sensual power of the Goddess within.'"

"Through cooking?" I asked.

"Yes. She says cooking is alchemy, and she's training us to be apprentice alchemists."

Two more women emerged from the house, laughing and chattering, clearly having a wonderful time.

"Is everyone okay to drive?" When they gave me odd looks, I clarified. "You shouldn't drink and drive."

This brought laughter from the group who headed for their cars. I pushed my way into the house and yelled, "Irma!"

The kitchen door swung open, and Irma appeared in a flowing pantsuit covered by an apron with her spiky hair in a turban. At least I was pretty sure it was Irma.

"What's going on?" I asked.

"What does it look like?" Irma said in her typical sassy attitude. "You said I could have a cooking class in your kitchen. Remember?"

"I thought you meant in a few weeks or months. How in the heck did you put this all together in days?" My irritation turned into awe. "I'm impressed."

"It's the wonder of the internet. I went viral. Can you believe it? Me?"

Zoe emerged from the kitchen and spotted Jennifer who hurried over to give her friend a hug.

"I bet this was your doing," Jennifer said to Zoe.

Zoe blushed. "Sort of. I mean, I put together the videos and uploaded them. But it was Irma's personality and charisma that everyone loved. We've already had almost a million views."

"Irma's personality?" I hesitated. "And charisma?"

Irma grinned. "If you got it, you got it."

I shook my head. "Girl, you got it all right."

IRMA AND ZOE FINISHED CLEANING UP IN THE KITCHEN while Jennifer and I took our things upstairs. When we returned, Irma had two champagne flutes waiting for us.

"I decided to make you French 75s, since I heard you liked them."

"Loved them," Jennifer reached for one of the flutes and took a sip, announcing it was, "Perfect!"

I had to agree, and when Irma offered samples of the results of the first cooking class, I gratefully accepted.

The four of us sat in front of the unlit fireplace as Irma set bowls of food in front of us along with a basket of biscuits.

"Is that…?" Jennifer's eyes widened. "Red beans and rice?"

"And sweet potato biscuits." Irma's voice was full of pride. "I've been trying to come up with the perfect recipe ever since you told me Chef Emile Toussaint was gone. Tell me what you think."

She didn't have to ask twice. We both dug in and didn't say a word until we took our last bites. The red beans and rice had just the right amount of smokiness and spice, and the biscuits were warm and flaky, even better with a generous pat of butter.

"Now you need to share the recipe with me," I said.

She chuckled. "It's online. I'll send you the link."

Irma was eager to hear about our adventures, and I wanted to share the story while it was still fresh. Her eyes widened and her mouth dropped open as Jennifer and I gave her all the details about our visit to New Orleans.

"But what about Sally?" Irma asked. "Did she get away with murder?"

"So far she has," I admitted, "but with Detective Azemar on her tail, I don't think it will be long before he gathers enough evidence to charge her. He's promised to keep me updated."

Irma shook her head slowly. "You two had quite the adventure, if you want to call it that. Food, sightseeing, and solving two murders, all in five days and four nights."

"When you say it like that," I said, "it does sound like a lot."

Zoe piped up. "Do you think George and Pearl will stay in New Orleans?"

"I have a feeling they might. Whatever their connection was to me, it seems to have been broken."

"Does that mean..." Jennifer spoke in a hush. "You're ghost-less?"

I looked around the room. It had been quite a while since there had been only living people in my home, and I had mixed feelings. Mostly I was happy for the peace and quiet.

"I believe I am." I raised my glass for a toast. "Here's to a future without any ghosts."

Jennifer's brows drew together. "Not even..."

"Who?" I asked. "Norma?" I'd completely forgotten about her. Norma had died in the house decades ago after she fell or more likely was pushed down the stairs. I'd also forgotten how much animosity Irma had toward the woman who stole away her fiancé and forced her to leave town to have her baby, Zoe's mother.

Irma scowled. "Who cares about that old biddy. In fact, I hope she's rotting in—"

The front door flew open, and an icy gust swept through the room, sending papers flying.

The lights on the chandelier flickered then went out.

"Irma." I looked around the darkened room. "When will you learn?"

THANK YOU FOR READING TEA IS FOR TALISMAN!

Will there be more Haunted Tearoom Mysteries? You'll have to wait and see!

Join Karen's Cozy Club for updates at https://karensuewalker.com or follow my Amazon page to get notified when I release my next book.

I also write the Bridal Shop Cozy Mysteries as well as the Arrow Investigations Humorous Action-Adventure Mysteries as KC Walker.

KEEP READING FOR RECIPES!

ELDERFLOWER CORDIAL

Yield: About 2 cups cordial base

Ingredients:

- 1 1/3 cups (270 g) sugar
- 1 1/3 cups (320 ml) water
- 1 cup (28 g) dried elderflowers or 3-4 cups (about 30-40 g) fresh elderflowers
- 1 lemon, sliced thinly
- 2 teaspoons (5 g) citric acid (optional, but helps preserve the cordial longer)

Instructions:

1. In a large saucepan, bring the water to a boil. Once boiling, remove from heat and stir in the sugar until fully dissolved to create a syrup. Allow to cool until lukewarm.
2. In a sterilized quart jar, add elderflowers, lemon slices, and (optional) citric acid. If using fresh elderflowers, you may need a second jar.
3. Pour warm syrup (sugar water) into the jar completely covering the flowers. Seal and shake to combine.

4. Refrigerate for 3-5 days, shaking once or twice a day.
5. Strain the mixture through a fine sieve or muslin cloth into a clean container. Cap with an airtight lid and refrigerate for up to three months. Without citric acid, it will last up to three weeks. Discard if the cordial turns cloudy.

To Serve:

- Pour about 2 Tablespoons of elderflower cordial into a champagne flute and top with sparkling water, Prosecco, or Champagne.

EASY RED BEANS AND RICE

Yield: 6 servings

Ingredients:

- 2 cups (370 g) uncooked white rice
- 2 Tablespoons (30 ml) olive or other vegetable oil, used 1 Tablespoon (15 ml) at a time
- 12-14 oz. (340-400 g) Andouille sausage, sliced into ½" thick rounds
- 2 medium yellow onions, diced
- 1 bell pepper, stemmed, seeded, and diced
- 3 celery sticks, diced
- 4 cloves garlic, minced
- ½ to 1 ½ Tablespoons Cajun seasoning (more if desired)
- 1 teaspoon salt
- ½ teaspoon black pepper
- 3 cans (15-16 oz. or 425-450 g) red kidney beans—2 drained, 1 pureed with its liquid
- 2 bay leaves
- 2 cups (455 ml) water or broth (chicken, vegetable, or beef stock or broth)
- Hot sauce for serving
- Parsley or green onions for garnish (optional)

Directions:

1. Prepare rice according to package directions.
2. Heat a large, heavy-bottomed Dutch oven or pot over high heat and add 1 tablespoon (15 ml) of olive oil. Once the oil is hot, add the sausage in a single layer. Let it cook for 1-2 minutes, then flip to brown the other side. Remove sausage from pan and set it aside.
3. Lower the heat to medium-low and add the remaining tablespoon (15 ml) of olive oil to the same pot. Stir in the diced onions, bell pepper, and celery and cook for 8-10 minutes, stirring frequently util soft. Add the minced garlic, Cajun seasoning, salt, and black pepper. Stir and cook for another minute.
4. In a blender or food processor, puree one can of red beans with the liquid from the can. Add it and the other two cans of drained red beans, bay leaves, and broth (or water) into the pot. Stir to combine everything, and if needed, add a bit more liquid. Bring the mixture to a low boil, then immediately reduce to low, cover, and simmer for 20 minutes.
5. Add the sausage back to the pot and simmer for another 5 minutes. Taste and adjust the seasoning with salt and pepper

as well as additional Cajun seasoning to taste.

6. Scoop about a cup of the beans and sausage into bowls and top with rice. Garnish with chopped parsley or green onions if desired and serve with hot sauce on the side.

SWEET POTATO BISCUITS

Yield: 30 biscuits

Ingredients:
2 1/2 cups (300g) flour
2 tsp baking powder
3/4 tsp salt
1/2 cup (115g) butter or other shortening
1 egg, well beaten
3/4 cup (180 ml) milk
1 1/2 cups (340g) mashed sweet potatoes (about
2-3 sweet potatoes) (see note)

Directions:

1. Preheat oven to 400°F (200°C)
    1. Sift flour, baking powder, and salt together in a large bowl, then cut in butter or shortening until mixture resembles coarse meal. (You can use a food processor for this step.)
    2. In another bowl, combine milk, egg and sweet potato mash, then combine with the flour mixture and blend until it's just moistened and holds together.
    3. Chill for 10 minutes (optional, but why not stop and have a cup of tea?)

4. Knead lightly 3-4 times on floured surface, then roll ½-1/3 inch thick.
5. Cut rounds with floured cutter and place on greased or parchment-lined baking sheet.
6. Brush tops with milk (optional, helps make the top golden-brown).
7. Bake at 400 F for 15 min. Makes about 30 biscuits.

April's note 1: To prepare mashed sweet potatoes, I like to boil the potatoes with their skin on until they're fork tender, about 40-50 minutes. Let them cool enough to handle and the skins will slide right off. If you want them cooked more quickly, peel and cut into 1" cubes and boil for 12-15 minutes. Either way they're cooked, drain and mash them with a fork, potato masher, or mixer.

April's note 2: When cutting out biscuits, try not to twist the cutter. Twisting will seal the edges, and the biscuits won't rise as nicely.

PECAN PRALINE COOKIES

Yield: 24 cookies

Ingredients:

- ½ cup (115 g) butter, softened
- 1 ½ cups (300 g) light brown sugar, packed
- 1 large egg
- 1 tsp vanilla extract
- 1 ½ cups (180g) all-purpose flour
- ½ tsp salt
- 1 cup (about 120 g or 4 oz.) chopped pecans

Directions:

1. Preheat the oven to 350°F (180°C) and grease a cookie sheet or line with parchment paper.
2. In a medium bowl, cream the butter, brown sugar, and egg together until light and fluffy by hand or using a mixer. Add the vanilla extract and mix in.
3. Add the flour, salt, and pecans and stir until there's no more dry flour. It will be a very firm dough.

4. Scoop out about 2 Tablespoons of dough and shape into balls.
5. Place the balls on the prepared cookie sheet. Flatten them to about 1/8 to ¼ inch thickness using the bottom of a glass or whatever you have handy.
6. Bake in a preheated 350°F (180°C) oven for 10 to 12 minutes, or the edges are browned.
7. Allow the cookies to cool on the baking sheet for a few minutes then transfer to a wire rack to cool completely.

NOTE FROM THE AUTHOR:

For all of Karen Sue Walker's books, visit https://karensuewalker.com. And while you're there, sign up for Karen's Cozy Club. You'll get about 42 emails a year with stories, recipes, promotions, contests, and giveaways!

Which series is your favorite?

- *Haunted Tearoom Cozy Mysteries*
- *Bridal Shop Cozy Mysteries*
- *Arrow Investigations Humorous Action-Adventure Mysteries by KC Walker*

Write me at karen@karensuewalker.com and let me know!

www.ingramcontent.com/pod-product-compliance
Lightning Source LLC
Chambersburg PA
CBHW061810190726
48289CB00007B/2150